The Journal of Unlikely Architecture is...
fresh and crisp, surreal and weird, highly
unlikely indeed.

— Lois Tilton, Locus Online

I thoroughly enjoyed Journal of Unlikely
Entomology. One wouldn't think you could
get far with an insect theme, but they do.
These are really good stories, not novelties.

— Sam Tomaino, SFRevu

If any zine today reliably offers tales that are
weird, it's this one.

— Lois Tilton, Locus Online

Wow, fantastic blog structure! How lengthy
have you ever been blogging for? you made
blogging glance easy. The total glance of
your site is great, as well as the content

— Comment from 74.91.27.26

Fact: Like magpies, **clowns** covet shiny objects.

Keep your **eyes** closed.

UNLIKELY STORY

Presents

CLOWNS:

THE UNLIKELY COULROPHOBIA REMIX

Edited by

Bernie Mojzes and A.C. Wise

Art Direction

Linda Saboe

Cover Art

Linda Saboe

Interior Art

Bryan Prindiville

Unlikely Story, LLC

Berwyn, PA

Unlikely Story presents:
   Clowns: The Unlikely Coulrophobia Remix

Cover Art copyright Linda Saboe.
Interior Art copyright Bryan Prindiville.

Editors: Bernie Mojzes and A.C. Wise
Art Direction & Web Site: Linda Saboe
Print/PDF layout: Bernie Mojzes

Published by Unlikely Story, LLC
46 Eastwood Road
Berwyn, PA 19312
http://www.unlikely-story.com

ISBN: 978-1-944597-00-9

Fact: Inside the **heart** of every clown lie three smaller clowns, **gnawing** their way out.

Table of Contents

Fact: The first clown is also the last clown. There is **always** a clown at the beginning, and a clown at the **end**.

Introduction
Between Writers and Clowns

by Robin Blyn

This is the scene:

After many years of labor, Paul Beaumont (Lon Chaney) has finally proven his theories about the origin of mankind. He believes that greatness awaits him. Yet when he arrives at "The Academy" to present his works, he finds that his patron, Baron Regnard (Marc McDermott), is in the process of presenting Paul's discoveries as if they are his own. When Paul interrupts the proceedings and insists that the Baron tell the members of "The Academy" that the theories and their proofs are actually his, the Baron dismisses him as insane. Paul protests, and here is when we arrive at the definitive moment in Victor Sjörström's *He Who Gets Slapped* (1924), for when the Baron responds by slapping Paul in the face, every grizzled and white-haired academician erupts in grotesque, unbridled laughter. The camera lingers on their faces, all of them contorted in cruel hilarity.

This is an expressionist dramatization of every writer's worst nightmare, for the writer is utterly exposed to ridicule. No matter what he writes, he will never be anything more than a joke. Sjörström's film takes this fear to its logical conclusion. From this point forward, Paul Beaumont abandons his inquiry into the origin of mankind and instead becomes a performer who revels in the hideous streak of sadism in human nature. Paul Beaumont becomes a professional clown, a clown whose entire performance consists in getting slapped by other clowns. Night after night, he re-enacts his humiliation, and every slap pushes the crowds to new levels of hilarity. However more youthful, the laughing faces in the audience are every bit as grotesque as the faces of the academic elders. Precisely because he has failed as a writer, Paul can perform the condition of writing itself: the condition of perpetual abjection.

In contrast to the audience in the film, *He Who Gets Slapped* invites its viewers to feel deep empathy for the clown. At the same time, the film evokes a kind of dread. We do not fear "He," as Paul Beaumont now calls himself; we fear *for* him because he is enmeshed in the dreamwork of our own anxieties. As a clown, "He" represents our own vulnerability to the cruel world, the suffering that is rendered all the more painful because no one will take it seriously, except as entertainment. In Sjörström's film, it is not so much that the clown suffers so that we don't have to, but that the clown suffers because we do. In the figure of Lon Chaney's clown, that suffering becomes a recognizable commodity, a profitable feature of the amusement industry. Part of the dread that the film evokes, then, is the clown's status as professional sufferer. It is a profession that depends upon the sadomasochist relationship between the performer and his audience; the clown's sadism is profitable only because of our own masochistic desires. Ineluctably, a troubling insight comes into view: If we identify with "He," we are also masochistically dependent upon the voracious crowds that facilitate our humiliation.

In *He Who Gets Slapped*, the dread that attaches itself to clowns is that they tell us too much about ourselves. The stories in this collection confirm Sjörström's insight. Therefore, they present as perfectly normal the complex fears that people have about clowns. From this perspective, there really is no such thing as "coulrophobia," if by that word we mean an abnormal fear of clowns. Thus this volume delivers precisely what it promises in its title: "unlikely coulrophobias" akin to the complex anxieties at work in *He Who Gets Slapped*. In the pages that follow, as in Sjörström's film, clowns are clever artists, participants in sadomasochistic rituals, and extant embodiments of truths we would just as soon forget.

The clown-as-artist emerges in the stories that playfully evoke the clowns that have populated horror films in recent decades. Kristen Roupenian's "Thou Antic Death," Line Henriksen's "Stilts," and Cate Gardner's "A Silent Comedy," all inventively satirize that genre. These stories, we can say, clown around with the idea of coulrophobia, and thereby they remind us that the clown has long served as a privileged figure for a particular kind of artist, a jester who challenges established norms, social and political hierarchy, and the most sanctified truths of a given historical moment. For this reason, the pervasive sentiment in this collection is that clowning is a dangerous business. This is most explicit in Virginia M. Mohlere's "A Million Tiny Ropes," but throughout the collection clowns exist in a state of physical or psychic danger.

As in Sjörström's film, the horror in these stories thus most often lies in the cruelty enacted upon the clowns themselves. In Chris Kuriata's "Whaling with Clowns," clowns are literally used as whale bait, and in Charles Payseur's "Pushpin and Pullpin," we witness rank physical brutality. In Dayle A. Dermatis's "Queen and Fool," by contrast, the suffering is more psychological; the fool is tortured by unrequited love. Like *He Who Gets Slapped*, but in a very different key, Derek Manuel's "Five Things Every Successful Clown Must Do" implies that the audience and the clown exact violence upon one another. Although Manuel's clowns turn out to be a tentacle-wielding species that feasts on human flesh, the story is a parable for the inhumanity of humans who feed off of the misery of clowns. Here I am reminded of the sadomasochism at the heart of Sjörström's film.

The violence done to Paul Beaumont is not limited merely to the slaps he receives, of course, but includes the silencing that they enforce.

Paul's voice will never be heard above the din of the laughter that follows from that first slap. Several stories in this collection similarly link the suffering of the clown to various forms of censorship. "Perfect Mime," by Sarah K. McNeilly, evokes the myriad historical attempts to mute the politically volatile performances of "jesters" and "fools." In her story, a female clown is utterly dehumanized, enslaved to the performance demanded by the men who control her. The "perfect mime" is a silenced woman, a victim of patriarchy's relentless gender norms. By contrast, in Carlie St. George's "Break the Face in the Jar by the Door," a creepy disease that turns a child into a clown ultimately allows her to break with social indoctrination. In this story, to become a clown is to become liberated, free from social and self-censorship. Likewise, "Mr. Boingo Saves the World," by J.H. Pell, celebrates the clown for his or her difference from the status quo, and a similar sense of the clown as rebel is at the heart of Jeff Wolf's "An Argument for Clowning on the Sabbath." As silenced dissident or triumphant rebel, the clown here is dangerous precisely because she or he reveals society as inherently repressive.

The culture industry, however, is what finally silenced clowns. For most of its history, clowning has entailed both visual and verbal art. In fact, there would have been no reason to censor clowns, if they had not been given to scathing commentary and pointed critique. By the turn of the century, however, competition within the culture industry prompted the emergence of the three-ring circus extravaganza we now associate with Barnum & Bailey. Here, under "The Big Top," the noise of simultaneous performances prohibited the clown's verbal art. Circus clowning became exclusively visual. By 1924, the year in which *He Who Gets Slapped* is released, the one-ring circus in which "He" performs is already long gone. Sjörström's film thus registers nostalgia for a bygone era in which clowns had a privileged place in the world of entertainment. Several stories in this collection share the film's melancholia, for they, too, fear that clowning is quickly disappearing from the contemporary world. On the brink of extinction, they imply, is something ineffably human — a sense of enchantment, perhaps, or even pointless silliness. Foremost among these stories is Holly Schofield's "A Distant Honk," which portrays clowns literally as an endangered species, threatened by human destruction of their "habitat." So, too, Cassandra Khaw's "Clown Shoes" is a melancholic sketch of the plight of discarded clowns. Other stories suggest the decline of clowns and clowning by linking them to death. This is true in Mari Ness's "The Game," in which we meet a clown in hospice playing chess with Death, and in Evan Dicken's "Melpomene's Heirs," where ghostly clowns attempt, however ineptly, to cheer a couple after the death of their child. The failure of the clowns signals their obsolescence, and thus the story links the disappearance of clowns with a fall into unmitigated mortality.

Taken together, these stories and others by Caroline M. Yoachim, T. Jane Berry, Joe Nazare, Chillbear Latrigue, Jason Arias and Karlo Yeager Rodriguez, suggest that we would lose a great deal more if clowns ceased to exist. At least in our art and in our imagination, they remain objects of unlikely coulrophobias that put us face to grease-painted face with some of the most unpalatable facets of human nature.

Robin Blyn

Author, *The Freak-garde: Extraordinary Bodies and Revolutionary Art in America*

Fact: Most species of clowns have teeth like **sharks;** they go all the way back.

Rarer clowns have baleen, but it isn't the krill they strain.

Five Things Every Successful Clown Must Do

by Derek Manuel

1. Understand the Humorous Nature of Tragedy

People have always found pleasure in the misfortune of others. You should understand that many people today dislike and mistrust clowns implicitly and will enjoy your suffering especially. Use this to your advantage by exploiting the blurry line between comedy and tragedy.

People will laugh if you lose your balance on a carelessly discarded banana peel. The greatest clown I ever met, Professor Nimrod, could slip, flail about and tumble to the ground, bounce on her backside, and land on her shoe bulbs, only to slip on the same peel again. It would have made Pratfall the Clumsy proud.

However, if you sever a tentacle and lose a great volume of ichor, the audience will have reactions ranging from shock to terror and nausea. That's not how you want your performance to end.

2. Have Confidence in Your Ability

To be a successful clown, you have to believe in your power to entertain and deceive. Remember that when you are performing for people, you are playing a character.

You should frequently make "eye contact" with members of the audience. This is one way to communicate your character's confidence in its plans before they fail for foreseeable reasons (e.g., stepping on the business end of a rake before releasing a pie). It can also express sadness (e.g., realizing that a handshake is not a peace offering, but merely an electrifying ruse).

Even though the eyespots on your cephalic tentacles don't really resemble human eyes on close inspection, the camouflage is sufficient at performance distances. My dear friend Professor Nimrod was able to secrete the perfect quantity of slime around her eyespots so that they glistened and shimmered in the low light of the bigtop.

It may be reassuring to realize that many humans are uncomfortable with prolonged eye contact and will look away quickly. Those who are too stupid to look away often make easy prey.

3. Use Props and Costume to the Fullest

You have to understand how your shoe bulbs change shape and size over the course of the season, in response to both your life cycle and variations in your diet. Chasing prey on shoe bulbs comically large enough to crush bones is pure folly, and not in a good way.

Use of the electric palm sucker and the florotoxin gland also require study and practice. Professor Nimrod and I once spent a lovely weekend savoring a captive human. We learned that different doses of florotoxin produce different effects on the primitive and poorly organized human nervous system. A demisquirt temporarily paralyzes the entire body. Two squirts yield powerful hallucinations resulting in shrieking terror, while three and a half squirts get you hysterical laughter. If you want to become as strong, flexible, beautiful, and curvaceous as my partner

Professor Nimrod was, you will need a balanced diet of both fearful and entertained flesh.

Never use more than four squirts of florotoxin. This will bring instant death to even the largest prey, and consuming the flesh of a dead human will plunge you into a profound depression.

4. Be Aware of Your Surroundings

Years ago, clowns could feed at circuses with impunity. Modern circuses are large commercial affairs, with audiences too big and diverse to sit idly by while you eat some of them. No matter how hungry you are, don't do it.

After the show, you can often catch a single family off-guard as their aging automobile refuses to carry them away with the rest of the herd. However, if you have fed in a circus parking area recently, it will be in your best interest not to do this again for some time. So how do you keep yourself alive while honoring our pact with the dread Order of Ringmasters?

Use your wings. Those things that cover your beak and get in the way when you're eating are called "suspenders" because they're made to suspend you in the air! Once you have selected your next meal at the circus, get to the highest position you can, jump off, and follow them home on the breeze. You are a clown. Act like one.

5. Construct an Inconspicuous Hive

I feel like this should be obvious by now, especially to those of you who are familiar with my history. But a growing contingent of clowns is actively spreading misinformation, so I'll debunk one of the most destructive myths you've probably heard.

The Old Fools Clan tells us that it's wrong to take more humans than strictly necessary to survive. They say we should live in the woods to avoid temptation and disguise our hives as things that occur in nature, like mushrooms or anthills.

Talking about this philosophy, I'm reminded of a joke. You've probably heard it before.

What happened to the happy, peaceful clown who expended all of her protein building a beautiful mushroom-shaped hive?

This is what happened to her. She came home one day and found some humans who had been hunting in the woods. The humans had found her huge mushroom and, being sentient life forms, knew that mushrooms don't get that big. They had beat on it and kicked it until the love of her life, Professor Nimrod, came out, and when they saw Professor Nimrod, they shot holes in her beautiful, strong wings. They hacked off her vibrant shoe bulbs with their hatchet and tore out her cephalic tentacles. And the happy, peaceful clown could do nothing but hide behind a tree and watch her lover's beak open and close, over and over, until it stopped. Then she felt like a filthy coward who didn't deserve to call herself a clown.

I got tired of being that joke. Now, I build my hive in the dark closet no one ever goes into, the dusty space under the bed, or the restroom with the flickering light. I eat anyone I want to eat, Ringmasters be damned. Almost everyone's been to a circus at least once.

Fact: It is impossible to **taxidermy** a clown. A clown may achieve & maintain a comparable state naturally. For centuries, if necessary.

Gags, Bits, and Business

by T. Jane Berry

The resident is about to gag. He presses himself against the wall, far from the body.

"Come here. So you can see."

He looks up, terrified, and slides a few feet forward.

"Tom, right?"

"Yeah," he says, trying not to take a breath, even though this decedent is only a couple of hours old. He smells of stale popcorn.

"Tom, I'm Dr. Marion Brandes." I extend my hand and feel the moisture on his palm through my latex gloves.

"A simple case. Circus comes to town and the clown drops dead during intermission. Bet it's a heart attack. Too many funnel cakes. Easy, right?"

Tom nods, his cheeks pinking up.

"First, the basics. Hit record on the tape. Male, six feet three inches, 213 pounds. Forty-three years old."

Someone knocks and swings the door open without waiting for an answer.

"Dr. Brandes?"

At first, I see a small child. I step in front of the body to block it from her view. I look closer. She is no child.

"You can't be in here."

"I'm with Giggles."

"Family waits outside."

Her eyes crinkle.

"Do I look like family?"

She does not. Her type of dwarfism is achondroplasia. Bowed legs and tiny limbs give away her genetics.

"I'm about thirty shades darker than Giggles."

And there was that, too.

"About his white makeup. I've been unable to remove it."

"It's not makeup," she replies, offering no explanation, instead holding out papers. "I have authorization to be present at his autopsy."

It's a living will that permits an Osmina Ransom to be Giggles' medical representative at his autopsy.

"Are you a physician?"

"I'm the magician. Here to facilitate."

"I don't need your assistance."

"Have you ever autopsied a clown?"

"Absolutely. Judy McGregor played a clown at our Fourth of July parade every year. She passed of kidney cancer in oh-six."

Osmina snorts.

"You haven't autopsied a real clown. I'll be here when you need me." She stands beside Tom, who is taking little shallow sips of air. I resume my narrative.

"The decedent's facial skin has been bleached white. Blue triangles are tattooed over and under each eye. Lips are red-rimmed. Cheeks have been artificially reddened—"

"It's supposed to look like sunburn," says Osmina, stroking his red hair reverently. "He's a happy hobo."

There is an object lodged in the left nostril. I tug on the end of it. A red scarf slides from his nose, then a yellow scarf, a blue scarf, a green scarf...

"Decedent's nasal cavity contains six joined scarves."

"Try this," says Osmina, sniffing Giggles' red wig and beckoning Tom to do the same. His expression changes from skepticism to delight.

"It smells like cotton candy... rain on hot asphalt... old cigarettes stubbed out in sand," he says.

Osmina smiles and I notice that she is holding Tom's hand.

"Focus on the checklist," I say, as much to myself as to Tom. I lift the hospital gown to examine the torso.

"There appears to be a condom or balloon over the decedent's genitalia."

I gently tug at the latex, but it does not come off.

"No, that's his. It's a balloon animal. A dachshund, if I remember right."

Tom and Osmina bury their faces in Giggles' hair and breathe deeply. I catch a whiff of cotton candy and greasepaint. The smell brings me back to the age of five, clutching a bag of roasted peanuts in one hand, my father's coat in the other... I shake my head and make a Y-shaped incision into Giggles' chest. His skin crackles like cellophane.

"What are those?" asks Tom, suddenly fearless, leaning into the body cavity.

"Those are the lungs."

I pull one out. It's pink and rubbery. It deflates with a flatulent sound. The odorless gas inside settles around us.

"Are they supposed to look like that?" asks Tom, his voice high and nasal.

"Helium. They're filled with it," I say. "Don't touch anything else."

Tom points to the spot where a liver should be.

"Is that—"

He reaches in, ignoring my order, and pulls out a candy apple by the stick.

"Tart granny smith," says Osmina, holding something else she's pulled from the cavity.

"Both of you back away from the table. This body has been tampered with."

Osmina holds it up to Tom's nose. He breathes in and moans slightly, opening his mouth. She places the red and white striped shard into his mouth. His face relaxes into bliss.

"It's like Christmas is inside of me..." he says, reaching into the chest opening to snap off another piece of peppermint rib.

"Stop... you're contaminating the body... the pathogens..." I stammer. The smell of sugar is overwhelming. I gag from it.

Tom lifts a smooth black sphere from the spot where we would usually find a heart. I turn toward the door for help, but the room tilts and whirls. I end up back where I started, leaning against the table.

Tom tips the sphere toward me. A printed triangle floats to the surface through purple water.

DROPSY
THE CLOWN

"What's this?" Tom asks, taking a bite from the apple. The red candy stretches down his teeth in points.

"That's your new name," says Osmina.

"Hrm," says Tom, chewing. "Sawdust in your nose... buttery stale popcorn... elephant dung..."

Osmina holds the door open and Tom follows, ball in one hand, candy apple in the other. I step forward to stop them and hit the floor instead. I watch their feet retreating down the hall. One set little, one set big.

"First, there is the business," she explains. "The little gestures that show the audience who you are..."

I wake up on the floor, coated in a fine dusting of powdered sugar. The exam table is empty. The recording has stopped. The tape has wound itself back to the beginning. I press play and hear my own voice.

"Male, six feet three inches, 213 pounds. Forty-three years old."

I hear Osmina's knock, and then my narration fades out. Instead, I hear a man shouting. His voice is faint, as if recorded from hundreds of feet away.

"Welcome, ladies and gentlemen, to the most spectacular show in the world..."

Fact: Clowns have no fewer than five **eyes** somewhere on their **bodies**. At any given time, at least three of them are **watching** you.

Mr. Boingo Saves the World

by J.H. Pell

"I'll go right home and get my things," he answers the girl with yellow beads in her hair. The only young person in the crowd who has offered him a smile instead of a sneer. "Clubs, hoops, balls, everything. Just a little later. Then I'll show you all the juggling I know." What's the harm in making promises on the day the world ends?

The girl hugs harder on an old lady shading under a hat the size of a Thanksgiving turkey platter. She bounces and chatters her excitement and a little thrill of pride gives an extra curve to the fat lines around his mouth. Then Granny meets his gaze with a narrow how-dare-you glare. His smile dies, halfway born.

He turns away and pushes through to the front. Can't stand the press of bodies on this hot July afternoon. Tar, sweat and cigarettes in the air, not even a breeze from the river. Paint on his face running with sweat. Wig starting to itch something fierce. Almost enough to make him want to take two more steps forward, into the too-deep, too-sharp shadow of the alien ship.

Almost.

Across an empty street, deep within that shadow, the Renaissance Center gleams darkly, the skyscraper more like his idea of a spaceship than the pustulent hurricane wheeling above it. So far, it is happening here in Detroit just the way the TV showed in New York, London, DC, Tokyo. The ship, the shadow, the waiting. Next come the flashes, the static, the dark. Then nothing.

The TV left out that when the shadow creeps over you it brings a hum, deep and grating, that cuts straight into your nerves.

No one in the crowd moves or makes a sound as the shadow engulfs them. The screaming starts when hunks, pods or something, tear free from the ship and fall.

An impact in the middle of the street raises a cloud of ozone and burning oil. Folks surge backwards, leaving him standing alone. Like a leader. Or a fool. But he's only old. If he had young legs, he'd run too.

The smoke sets him coughing, then parts to reveal a patch of deeper dark. A stuttering, sibilant shriek jabs out from it. A moment later, a flat voice follows.

"People of Earth," it says. "Rejoice, for salvation is at hand. You will know the peace of the Eyeless God—"

It goes on and on like that. Halfway familiar. Maybe out in space they watched the same old B-movies he grew up on. He can almost smell the mingled aromas of popcorn and exhaust, almost hear the canned scream of some white lady, just out of time with her demise on screen. Almost feel his date's leg pressing on his.

Been a while.

Someone behind him gasps. While his mind has been wandering, a seam of light has split the pod. He half expects a robot man to step out and start up with the *klattu barada something-something*.

What slides out instead is a cross between an elephant, an octopus, and a jello dessert. Like the ship, it is in constant motion. Rippling tendrils sprout from it and recede. Backlit, restless blobs churn within. Its seaweed stench takes him all the way back to a childhood spent combing Carolina beaches.

A mottled, hairy orb fills its peak. A dark lentil within the orb pans past him and around, and then past him again. And then it snaps back and his spine prickles with sudden sweat and he knows that the alien is staring at him, just as he is staring at it.

His stomach lurches. He wishes he had stayed home. Dying with his face on seemed like a better idea a couple of hours ago. His mouth has gone dry as an empty bucket.

The alien's sproutings become violent. Half of the floating bits clot around the eye, and the other half push at the outer membrane like they just smelled a stink inside.

A tuneless squawk, then the tin voice says: "No."

And he knows, he *knows*, what he sees in that dark and glittering, jittering eye. His blood hums, fear calling to fear across an unfathomable gulf of space and species.

Thirty years of backyard birthday parties. Thirty years of inconsolable tears where he tried to bring joy.

Enough.

He does a quick two-step, whips out his arms, opens his eyes wide to the whites and paints on the biggest, baddest, meanest smile he ever practiced in the gloom of a bitter, hung-over dawn. He reaches for his screechingest, shrillest, worst-of-all voice. He shouts. "I-i-i-i-t's me! Mi-i-i-i-i-ster Boingo!"

The alien jerks. The pod hisses and spits. "No. Reaver. Render. Salter of Souls," the voice says. "Boiler. Toothed Maw of Hell. No. No. No."

It convulses, ruptures, puddles to scabs and ooze. A dead jellyfish torn by gulls.

His hands shake and his heart seems about to beat itself to pieces, but he finds that he can walk. He steps up to the beached eye, half-gagging on the stench, and raises his foot as high as his old hips allow. His knee pops.

Thirty years.

He stomps down with one ludicrous, flopping shoe.

A blue-white bolt bleaches the shadow. He looks up, shading his eyes with a gloved hand. The light is only on him. In the spotlight at last, old man. It winks out as suddenly as it came.

As he blinks away the after-image, the whirling ship dismantles into smaller and smaller pieces. Soon a sooty rain begins to fall.

Starts to seem like the world might make it to dinner. So he leaves, girl and Granny in tow. They walk with him through streets of sagging foreclosures and whole blocks reclaimed by prairie. They wait on his porch while he rummages for his kit. By the time he emerges, Granny has cranked up an emergency radio. Crackling, accented voices relay reports of empty skies and black rain from cities around the world.

He takes his battered old clubs from his bag, gives one a flip. Does a shuffle. Puts on a good smile this time. The girl huddles on his steps, wide eyed and grinning, as the clubs take to the air.

FACT: Approximately 7% of clowns are hollow.

Fact: The camera really does **steal** a
piece of the clown's **soul**.
That's why they perform in public.
They don't want it anymore.

An Argument for Clowning on the Sabbath

by Jeff Wolf

"Can one clown on the Sabbath?" Chaim asked Moishe.

Moishe stroked the outline of his chin and studied the white grease that accumulated on his fingertips.

"Certainly one can," he said. "Just as one with a rifle and a campsite by the coast can shoot an osprey — then pluck its feathers, boil the meat with scallions, and serve it at a briss."

Chaim faced away to hide his eye roll, but he turned into the mirror and met Moishe's gaze once more. "*Should* one clown on the Sabbath?" he said.

Moishe leaned back in his chair, bare-chested save for the suspenders holding up his red-and-white striped pants. "That depends on the one who presumes to clown."

"Let's say it's you and I who presume."

"Let's indeed."

Chaim approached the mirror. Beneath the line of filament bulbs, sweat beaded on his forehead. He snatched a glass jar from the ledge and popped loose the lid. "So you have no objection?" he said, scooping two thick fingers of red grease and smearing a wide streak above his left eye.

"Surely I object. We are professional clowns, and the Torah forbids working on the Sabbath."

Moishe rose, walked to the costume rack, and removed two silk vests. After a moment of careful study, he dropped one to the floor and laid the other, blue with white polka dots, over his chair.

Moishe stared at Chaim through the mirror. Stage makeup gave Moishe's face a saccharine grin, but his true features sat patient and neutral. Chaim felt the grease slipping between his eyebrow hairs. He relented and recited his usual part.

"But surely some men may ply their trade on the Sabbath? Consider the deli owner who makes sandwiches. All week long, never leaving his feet, and on his one day of rest he would be forbidden by G-d to prepare *himself* a sandwich?"

"Surely G-d is not so cruel!" Moishe proclaimed.

Chaim resumed spreading makeup, content the exercise had ended. He closed the loop around his left eye, then the right.

"But," Moishe said. The word fell swift and heavy, like leaden clown shoes. "But is not the deli man, by making sandwiches only for himself, doing so merely in an amateur sense?"

Chaim stopped and lowered his hands. Across the room, Moishe donned a shirt with frilled cuffs and fastened the buttons. "After all, any man who makes a sandwich for his own enjoyment cannot be called a professional sandwich maker. Would you not agree?"

Chaim's accentuated eyebrows rose in sudden distress. Their discussion repeated itself often, but it had never continued this far.

"Would you not agree?"

Chaim opened his mouth but said nothing. He nodded.

"Similarly, any man may clown for his own amusement," Moishe said. "Which differs distinctly from clowning before an audience."

Chaim squeezed his red nose — an exercise Moishe taught him for regaining composure. "Can one, in fact, clown solely for one's own enjoyment?" he said.

Moishe sighed. He set his wig down in the chair and began unbuttoning his shirt. "Clowning for one's own amusement differs distinctly from clowning *purposely* for an audience," he restated.

His offer rejected, Chaim felt his frustration rising. "So what if it does?" he said. "The show must go on."

Moishe held a long, disappointed stare. Then his posture withered. Eyes downcast, he reached beyond the costume rack and pulled a rag, brown and fraying, from the elbow of a low-hanging pipe. He gave Chaim one last, sad look, then raised the rag to his face.

Chaim's eyes widened with horror. "Wait!" he shouted.

Moishe's hand froze. A powdering of white clung to the fibers of the rag.

"But if we clowned for an audience... on accident?"

Moishe's eyes brightened. "And how would such a situation transpire?"

"Suppose we are in your house, in private, clowning on the Sabbath simply for the love of clowning?"

"Go on," Moishe said.

"Unbeknownst to us, a gentile walks by on the sidewalk. He sees us through the window and starts laughing uncontrollably."

"Given our high clowning skill, certainly he would," Moishe said.

"Other gentiles on the street become curious and investigate this spontaneous laughter. Upon seeing us through the window, they start laughing as well."

"And, of course, we are ignorant to all of this."

"More onlookers arrive. Soon, a circus-sized crowd has formed outside your window. All rolling with laughter at a performance we did not know we were giving. Have we sinned?"

"I must believe we have not," Moishe said, holding out a shirt.

Chaim grabbed the fabric, but Moishe's hand stuck. "But if we clowned under the Big Top on the Sabbath, surely we would notice *that* audience, and as such would be obligated to cease clowning."

Chaim raised an exaggerated red eyebrow. "Suppose we are clowning with such passion that we lose all sense of our surroundings? Those who practice their arts with intense concentration often reach such a heightened state. Surely a clown as accomplished as yourself has experienced this?"

Moishe smiled and released his grip on the shirt. "I must admit that I have," he said. "It is as you say. All other things fall away, and only you and your clowning partner remain. The audience could be full of six-eyed cherubim and you would never know."

Chaim faced the mirror. Dipping a small finger in the grease, he touched up the red around his mouth. "Suppose we begin clowning on the Sabbath simply for the love of it. We then reach a state of focus so intense that we lose track of our surroundings, and while in that state, an audience arrives — an audience we thus have no knowledge of. Wouldn't it then be possible for us, professional clowns as we are, to clown on the Sabbath without sinning?"

"This logic is as sound as if it came from Rabbi Hillel himself," Moishe said. He adjusted his giant bowtie and they walked to the stage.

❀

Fact: A **drowned** clown in a swimming pool will always end up with its **feet** pointing east.

Fact: If you play a
recording of a
clown's voice
backwards it sounds
exactly the same.

'Thou Antic Death':
The Killer Clown
in Culture, Theory, and Practice

by Kristen Roupenian

A Thesis Submitted in Partial Requirement for the Degree of
Master of Science in Criminology
University of Maine, Bangor

September 2014

*In the parodical legends and the fabliaux the devil is the gay
ambivalent figure expressing the unofficial point of view, the material
bodily stratum. There is nothing terrifying or alien in him...*
—Mikhail Bakhtin, *Rabelais and His World*

SERVANT
O, my dear lord, lo, where your son is borne!
Enter Soldiers, with the body of JOHN TALBOT
TALBOT
Thou antic death, which laugh'st us here to scorn...
—William Shakespeare, *Henry VI Part 1*

ABSTRACT

This thesis argues that the growing prevalence of murderous, evil, and otherwise frightening clowns in the popular culture of the 1970s and 1980s led to a corresponding rise in the use of clown identifiers (costuming, make-up, and props) in the paraphilias of the serial killers who came of age during that period. It offers this

31

as the primary explanation for the statistically anomalous and yet apparently disconnected "clown murders" that began surfacing across the country in the mid-2000s and continue into the present day.

The thesis consists of three parts: first, a literature review, confirming the rise of the "scary clown" phenomenon during the 1970s and after (with special attention paid to cultural and media representations of the original 'killer clown,' John Wayne Gacy); second, a quantitative analysis of relevant murder cases over the past decade, which establishes a highly unusual rate of clown-related signifiers present at crime scenes; and third, a case study based on a series of in-depth interviews with David Michael Allan, a.k.a. 'Maccus the Clown,' who was, at the time of those interviews, incarcerated in the Maine State Prison facility in Warren, having been convicted of the murder of seventeen pre-teen boys while dressed in a clown costume. 'Maccus the Clown' strongly endorsed the argument presented in this thesis, locating the source of his own deviance in a single late-night TV movie he watched as a child.

Overall, the results of the study suggest that not only has this generation of serial killers been profoundly shaped by the consumption of evil-clown-related media during childhood, but that as the cohort born in the late 1970s reaches its late forties (the age of peak activity among paraphilia-driven serial killers) the frequency of these murders can only be expected to increase.

ACKNOWLEDGEMENTS

The average master's thesis in criminology requires only three years to complete; this one has taken nearly ten. When I first began this project, I conceived of it as an entirely research-based analysis. However, when David Michael Allen was first apprehended in Sagadahoc County, less than an hour from campus, my advisors — Wendy Graham, Lina Michaelson, and Kenneth Nee — suggested that I incorporate a case study element into the project. At the time,

I felt unable to refuse such an opportunity. Without my advisors' rigorous intellectual guidance, I would only ever have encountered Maccus the Clown from the safe remove of a university library. I would therefore like to acknowledge all three of my advisors for their unparalleled mentorship, as well as for their assistance in navigating the university bureaucracy when circumstances required me to take extended leave from the program.

My partner, Jason, has provided me with invaluable emotional, financial, and practical support over the past decade. Without his love and forgiveness, I would not have survived the process of writing this thesis. I thank him from the bottom of my heart.

The law enforcement agencies in both Warren and Bangor have been unstinting in their assistance to myself and my family. The round-the-clock protection they provided myself, my partner, and my son in the aftermath of David Michael Allen's escape was not, in the end, sufficient, but their willingness to provide it — and their kindness in the aftermath of tragedy — has not been forgotten. They too have sacrificed.

Although a day has not gone by when I have not regretted allowing Maccus the Clown into my life, I cannot but admit that from the first day we met, he did what I asked — he told me the truth about himself and his desires. Through his words, recorded here, we may see into the coming darkness.

This thesis is dedicated to my son, Daniel, in loving memory.

Danny, I'm sorry.

❁

Fact: The average clown goes through a metric ton of greasepaint in a lifetime. Greasepaint comes in a variety of tones to **mimic** human skin.

Everyone's a Clown

by Caroline M. Yoachim

When Amelia turned six, I took her to the circus. She'd been a little withdrawn lately, and I wanted to cheer her up. She watched with a grim expression as elephants marched around the ring. "What's the matter?"

"The elephants look unhappy."

I couldn't see anything wrong with the elephants, and the spotlight shifted to a trio of clowns. "Look at the clowns, Meelie, see the big red smiles?"

"You can see their faces? Do you like them?"

"Sure," I said, baffled by her odd response. I stared at the clowns. Amelia mumbled something and touched my arm to get my attention. Her face was painted like a clown — a bright red mouth and paper-white skin, black triangles above and below her eyes.

The woman in the next seat had clown make-up too, and a bright red wig. I scanned the audience. Every single seat was occupied by a clown. Sad clowns, happy clowns, scary clowns, nothing but clowns as far as I could see in the dim light. It had to be a trick, part of the act.

The show continued, and every performer was a clown. Amelia spent more time looking at me than at the stage. I tried to pretend that nothing was wrong so she wouldn't worry.

"Not long after the circus, my daughter turned into a sad clown, with a blue teardrop beneath her left eye," I told the neurologist. Dr. Williams was a silly clown, with a big red nose and high-arched eyebrows. Her rainbow hair framed her face in tight ringlets. I wondered what she looked like to other people.

"I'm amazed you can recognize people," she said.

"Everyone's a clown, but they aren't all the *same* clown."

She studied my MRI results. "There's nothing physically wrong with your fusiform gyrus, or anywhere else on the scan."

"What else can we try?" I asked. I needed to stop seeing clowns. I worried that my break with reality was what made my daughter so sad. We never should have gone to the circus.

"Maybe a psychiatrist?" Dr. Williams suggested. She gave me a referral.

"Midnight was sick all over the carpet," Amelia reported when I got back from my appointment. She had two tears under her left eye. That was a bad sign. People's clown faces didn't change for passing moods.

"I'll clean it up." Midnight's favorite cat pastimes were eating grass and puking on the carpet. I sprinkled a box of baking soda over the befouled area. "Is everything okay at school?"

Amelia nodded.

"Are you worried about something?" I asked. Amelia struggled with putting her feelings into words, as kids often do. Hell, grownups too. But I had to figure out why her clown face was so sad.

"Do you know what your face looks like?" she asked.

My heart sank. It was me, then. I'd been avoiding mirrors, but I didn't want Amelia to worry. In the most cheerful voice I could muster, I said, "Let's go look together at the mirror."

That was a mistake.

My too-big mouth was filled with pointy teeth and my eyes were bloodshot red with black pupils. I searched the face in the mirror for any feature that I recognized, any sign of what I'd looked like before my brain started distorting faces, but all I saw was a terrifying clown. I remembered that Amelia was standing beside me. Thank God she couldn't see what I saw.

"What's the matter with my face?" I asked.

"You used to be such a happy clown, and now you look scary. You look like worry and fear."

I didn't bother with the psychiatrist. If Amelia was seeing clowns, it had to be genetic. Or contagious, but I didn't even want to think about that. We sat down and talked, and she told me that her teacher was a sad clown, and the other kids were happy or silly or sad or scared. I asked her when she started seeing clowns, and she said she'd always seen them, she just hadn't known they were clowns until we went to the circus.

"I see clowns too," I told her, "and I'm worried because your clown looks sad."

"I don't like seeing everybody's inside feelings," Amelia said. "Have you looked at the cat?"

"Midnight?" The cat seemed fine, perched on top of the bookshelf. "She looks okay to me. What do you see?"

"I don't want to share it with you," Amelia said. "I think you don't like seeing the clowns."

"You didn't make me see clowns," I reassured her, "It was something about the circus—"

"No," Amelia said. "It was me. I thought you wanted to see what I saw."

I didn't really believe her, but I didn't want her to feel bad. "Okay, no problem. I see what you see, but not the cat. Let's share that too."

She touched my cheek, and one of her clownface tears faded away. Seeing clowns wasn't so bad. I could deal with a clown-cat if it would make my little girl happier.

I looked up at Midnight.

Perched on the bookshelf was a cat-sized spider, with beady black eyes and hairy legs. I flinched, but managed not to scream. "Has she always looked like that? I mean, to you?"

Amelia shook her head. "I think she's sick."

"We'll take her to the vet."

The vet was a tired-looking clown with faded blue hair. The waiting room was full of hideous creatures — dog-sized maggots and featherless birds and a guinea pig that didn't have a face. Amelia was completely unfazed, and sat with our giant spider-cat on her lap.

This was my new world, her world, full of horrifying animals and clown faces.

A happy clown came out of the treatment room with an ordinary-looking dog. I hoped the vet could cure our cat. I hated spiders. I almost wished I hadn't volunteered to see what Amelia saw. Then I saw her contented little clown face. If sharing these nightmarish visions was what it took to make her happy, I wouldn't flinch away.

I stroked one of Midnight's furry legs and tried to pretend the hissing noise was a purr.

Fact: Like **rabbits**, one day a year,
clowns lay brightly colored **eggs**,
hiding them, cuckoo-style,
in otherwise **ordinary** baskets.

Fact: A clown's **smile** continues to grow
for 6-8 weeks after **death**.

The Game

by Mari Ness

Death and the clown watched each other over the table.

They were playing chess.

The clown was no good at the game — she had spent her life focusing on contortionism, juggling and balloons. Neither, truthfully, was Death, who had never been one for tricks or games. But they had time, and they had the game before them, and so Death had moved a pawn, and invited the clown to move.

"This would be easier if I could remember how the knights move."

Death didn't crack a smile. "You should not give away your weaknesses to your opponent."

"My weaknesses." Her huge red gloved hand tried to move a bishop three squares, knocking three pieces over in the process. Death quietly picked up the pieces. "So, what, I'm not supposed to disclose the ovarian cancer or the fact that even now I'm trying not to throw up?" She moved the red gloved hand over the bishop again. "Anyway, I figured you knew all that stuff."

"No," Death said quietly. "We're not told why we're here. Just that we're here."

"We?"

"There are many Deaths, although we are all Death."

"Well. That's not creepy at all. Do you ever run into each other at the hospice here and decide to get a cup of coffee?"

"Not all of us like coffee."

"Not getting any less creepy. Are you planning on moving?"

"I'm trying to decide," Death said. A grey finger hovered over the table.

"You know, the funny thing is, I used to come here all the time. Cheer people up during their last moments, all that. Kids especially. Never saw you though." The clown moved a piece. Death raised one eyebrow; the clown sighed and moved the piece back. "You probably saw me, though. Didn't you?"

Death said nothing.

"Couldn't stand it, to be honest. But it paid well, and I thought — well, I thought maybe I was doing some good. To make up for everything else. It's not like the Peace Corps or being a nun or—"

Around the clown's eyes, the white paint grew a bit smudged. More skin appeared.

"And here I am, not able to give myself a laugh. Well. It's all kinda grim." She looked over at Death. "Get it? Grim? Grim Reaper?" She sighed. "Tough crowd."

"I have met with clowns before," Death whispered.

The clown pulled out three small red balls, balancing them in her hands. One went up; she tried to catch it, and missed. She reached into her pocket for a fourth ball. She looked at it for a moment. Her glance turned to the figure slouched in a chair in a corner.

"What's going to happen to Rachel?" she whispered.

Death fingered a chess piece.

"Oh come on," the clown argued, clutching the balls. "You can tell me. I'm dying anyway."

Death moved a bishop five squares.

"Please," she whispered.

"I don't know the future. Only the present."

"But you're Death."

"And thus focused on the past."

"Look," the clown said, fumbling with the balls. "I'm— ok, I'm not ok with this. I want more time. I need more time. I hate this. I hate you. But—"

A ball dropped to the floor.

"I think I can handle this if you tell me she's going to be all right."

"Your move."

"Do you do this with everyone? Come in and play games with them and refuse to answer questions?"

Death didn't answer.

"She put my face on today. Did you know that?"

A grey finger tapped the chess board.

"Oh, god. Ok then. This piece—" she touched the rook, "—it goes diagonal, right?"

"Forward."

The clown moved the piece two squares forward.

"I want to juggle again."

"Look at the board."

"Why me?"

Death moved a finger over several pieces.

"It was because I was juggling, right? When you showed up? That's why I'm getting—" She waved her hands in the large, dramatic gestures she had practiced for so long, wincing at the resulting pain. "This."

Death removed the clown's queen.

"I don't know why I did that. Just— I wanted to make them fly, one last time, you know?"

Death nodded.

"I could do that. Not anything else. But I could do that." She looked at the board. "Do we just keep playing until you take all my pieces?"

Another nod.

The clown shut her eyes and clutched the table for a moment, then opened her eyes again. "It's not to extend my time. I promise. It's just— I think I'd like to juggle again. If that's ok."

She didn't wait for an answer, turning from the table towards the floor and the balls scattered around her feet. The room spun and dipped. She ignored it. She could do this. She lowered herself gently to the floor. She'd done much more, when she was a clown. She could reach the balls, without moving much. Without calling for aid and having someone inject crap in her again, or upsetting Rachel. She could reach the balls. She could. There — one of them. Right there. Right there at the edge of the pool of blood—

The pool of blood that had not been there at the start of the game, the blood that now filled the corner of the room. The pool of blood with a figure slumped over it.

A figure with long, deep cuts on her skin.

The clown opened her mouth. But she could not scream.

She would not scream.

She turned towards Death, shaking.

"You weren't here for me. You were never here for—"

Death stepped forward, put a grey finger on her cheeks, on the tears running through her face paint.

The way she had once touched children, waving balloon animals, as they cried.

The room was very cold.

"Thank you for the game," Death said, picking up a pawn, and leaving.

Fact: You know of elephant graveyards.
There are clown graveyards as well.
Clowns aren't what's **buried** there,
but they still go to mourn.

Melpomene's Heirs

by Evan Dicken

The clowns kept trying — after the cancer had spread, after the doctors had given up, even after Charlie died. They had to have followed Becky back from the children's ICU. It makes me a little sick to imagine them crushed into my wife's van, eyes wide in painted hollows, gloved hands pressed to their mouths like children trying to hold in a secret. I know they're famous for squeezing into things, but I feel like, even numb as I was, I would've noticed a dozen manic grins glinting from the rearview mirror of my Prius.

They didn't have to hide. I bet Becky never even glanced back.

I first noticed the clowns at the funeral. They were in the rear, huddled in the shadow of the choral balcony, plaids and polka-dots swapped for somber black, their faces inked with tears and wide, grieving frowns. If a shock of electric blue hair peeked from behind a mourning veil, or one of them occasionally paused to consult a comically large pocket watch, no one seemed to notice. When I asked Becky if she thought we should ask them to leave, she just shrugged and looked away.

There were big plastic daisies and daffodils mixed in amongst the roses we threw onto Charlie's coffin. I was going to pick them off, but noticed the spray nozzles just in time to keep from ruining my good suit.

The pranks went on for a few weeks, at least while our friends were still trying to be supportive and the mailbox was brimming with sympathy. I'd season my eggs only to find they'd unscrewed the top of the shaker or replaced the salt with sugar. Once, they put fake spiders into the tub while Becky was taking a shower. I found her there about an hour later, naked and shivering in water long since run to cold. She didn't say anything, just stepped over the tangle of glistening black bodies and toweled off like nothing was the matter.

The whoopee cushions and chattering teeth weren't so bad, but the balloon Charlie was pretty tasteless. I knew Becky would never say anything, so I had a good shout one night, yelling about how the clowns were ruining our marriage. It felt good.

Things quieted down a bit after that, although I still saw oversized shoe prints in the flower beds and the occasional smudge of greasepaint on the bathroom mirror.

Becky and I drifted through the house, suddenly so big, so quiet. We ate together, slept in the same bed, went on long walks, unconsciously preserving the distance that had once been bridged by small hands. Eventually, summer ended and we went back to work. Although Principal Lee said it was alright if we took a leave of absence, neither of us wanted to stay home.

The kids were fine, if a bit subdued. I recognized a few faces from birthday parties and soccer games. Principal Lee wouldn't have put Charlie in my or Becky's class, but our son was the right age.

The clowns seemed subdued as well. Sometimes, I thought I heard a distant bicycle horn or exaggerated giggle rising up through the babble of children's voices, but nothing more. I started to think I'd gotten through to them, that they finally understood there was nothing they could do to help us.

When we got home, the house was full of feathers. Down covered the floor like thick snow, piled up around the couch and chairs in knee deep drifts. The AC kicked on, sending flurries of feathers swirling up from the vents. Becky went into the bathroom and locked the door. Knocks got no response, neither did pleading. I stood in the hall, forehead pressed to the cool wood of the door. I wanted to kick the damn thing down, but went for a drive instead.

I stopped to buy some whiskey at the Kroger near the soccer field where Charlie had scored his first goal. I've never been much of a drinker, but it seemed like the right thing to do. The store felt carnival bright, so I grabbed some bottom-shelf stuff in a big plastic bottle with a picture of a cowboy on the front and fled back into the humid dark.

Becky was in the living room when I got home. She'd swept most of the feathers into the kitchen and was sitting on the couch looking out the big picture window. I felt a flash of embarrassment when she glanced at the whiskey. I'm not sure what I'd wanted — anger, tears, relief, anything really. Instead, she just patted the cushion next to her. I sat and we passed the bottle back and forth for a while.

There were two clowns outside the window, one big and one small. They were making a show of trying to put a board into our shed that was far too long to fit. As much as I hated them in that moment, I had to admit the choreography wasn't half bad. They must've practiced for days.

Becky got up and came back with a couple of family albums. The clowns had drawn all over the pictures, giving us moustaches, black eyes, and missing teeth — nothing vulgar, though.

There was a picture of Charlie on his last birthday. Becky and I were holding him up to blow out the candles. With his cheeks puffed out and the light glittering in his eyes he almost looked like he had before the leukemia hollowed him out. The clowns had drawn a halo over Charlie's party hat and sketched great angel wings on his shoulders, spread as if to lift him from the hospital bed and away into the open sky.

"How could he slip away?" Becky gave a little hitch. "We held him so tight."

When I reached for her she didn't pull back, and we held each other for a while.

Through long overdue tears I saw the clowns approach. They crowded the picture window, chalk white faces pressed to the glass, their eyes bright as stars.

For once, I couldn't tell if they were laughing or crying.

Fact: Seven **species** of clowns have flowers in their lapels. The flowers are not worn, they are grown. They do not squirt water, but **tears**.

Break the Face in the Jar by the Door

by Carlie St. George

Tuesday mornings go like this:

Get up at 5:00. Don't wake your husband, who doesn't appreciate early mornings the way you've grown to. Get dressed. Apply makeup. Keep everything tasteful, classy. Nothing men might take as a silent invitation.

Downstairs, read the book you've hidden behind the laundry detergent. Your Me-Time: a precious 45 minutes with nothing but spaceships and explosions. The kind of thing you read in school, before you became a Wife and a Mother and a Bank Manager and a Real Adult. Then stow the book away, climb the stairs carefully. Skip the sixth step entirely — it creaks.

Open McKenna's door. Step over her Barbies, her toy microscope. She's a stomach sleeper, limbs spread like a starfish. Say her name, which will merit no reaction. Gently pull her toward you. Tickle her awake.

This is how Tuesday mornings go, how all school days go. Monotony is good. A break in the routine — like when you put on too much eye makeup or wear a shirt he doesn't like, when you're caught doing something childish or wake him climbing the stairs — this is how bad days begin. This is how you bring them on yourself. Say you'll stop doing this someday. Lie.

It's Tuesday again.

McKenna does not respond to her name. Pull her towards you. Notice, too late, how curly her ginger hair has become. See the unnatural whiteness of her skin, the too-vibrant red of her mouth, how her lips pull into an exaggerated frown that human lips are incapable of making. How red runs from under her eyes, like tears, like blood. Like greasepaint. How none of it smears away when she stirs under your panicked hands.

"Mommy?" McKenna says.

Break the routine. Shatter it. Scream.

Do not attack the doctors when they offer statistics instead of reasons, counseling instead of cures. Do not pretend to be an authority on coulrodermatism. Do not bite your neighbor's head off for calling it 'that creepy clown disease.' Do not yell at your friends for their stupid suggestions. Do NOT make a scene.

Apologize when your husband does all of these things.

The appointment with the child psychologist is at 10:00. Tell yourself you're not angry your husband refuses to go. Lie.

Dr. Huerta is not afraid to shake McKenna's too-white hand. Decide you like her, even if she ends up saying this is all your fault. Because it is your fault. It must be. Don't lie, not about that.

Don't cry when McKenna says, "Daddy hates my face." Don't cry when she says, "Maybe it's because I'm bad."

Stop crying. STOP. Tell her that she's perfect.

Blink when McKenna says, "Sometimes, I like it better this way."

Do not tell your husband what McKenna said.

It's your Me-Time. Read blogs detailing life with coulrodermatism. Lurk on community forums debating makeup versus surgery versus acceptance. Look at before and after pictures. Take particular notice of the children, the ones with red noses and wide, impossible grins.

Remember the question Dr. Huerta asked. Remember how it didn't even occur to you.

McKenna, why do you think your new face is so sad?

The plastic surgery consult is at 2:00 p.m. Do not argue with your husband. Do not let your horror at the thought of someone taking a knife to your six-year-old's face stop you from considering all the options.

Listen to the doctor say McKenna will need multiple surgeries. Listen to her explain how she'll apply permanent makeup with a tattoo gun. Listen to her say, "With time, I'm confident your daughter will pass for normal again."

Make a scene.

He's furious, of course. You're embarrassing him in public. You're being unreasonable. Why are you doing this to him?

Do not tell him he's an ass. Do not say, "This isn't about you." He won't understand those words, and really, whose fault is that? Instead, tell him McKenna is just a child. Remind him how much pain she'll be in daily. List all the potential side effects. Ask him what lesson she'll learn from this: will she think her parents don't love her if she's different? Will she came to hate herself inside and out?

Tell yourself he cares about these things. Tell yourself he's just scared. Tell yourself he can see reason.

Stop lying. Just stop.

The Bad Day becomes a Bad Week. He alternates sullen silence with interrogation. Don't you see how hard he tries? Don't you know you're all he has?

He doesn't hit you. He's never hit you. That's not the fear that's made you stay.

Don't cry when he starts crying. Don't chase after him when he leaves, promising to hurt himself if you don't love him, if you don't need him anymore. Remember he's never kept this promise or any other. Lock the door behind him. Try to sleep.

Never forget what McKenna said to Dr. Huerta.

"I was sad a lot cause Mommy was sad. But Daddy would get angry, so I tried to smile. But now, now I can't pretend. It's easier that way. My face just says what it wants to say."

Ask yourself: what would your face say, if you let it?

It's Tuesday again.

Get up. Don't wake your husband, passed out on the couch. You didn't hear him come home. Tell yourself you're sorry he's alive. Lie.

Get dressed. Apply makeup. Not classy — what you used to wear in school, when you didn't hide your books from anybody. White foundation. Black lipstick. Dark lines like razor cuts over your eyes.

Break the routine. Shatter it. Open McKenna's door and tickle her awake.

"Mommy, you changed too."

Try to respond to that. Fail. Settle for taking her shopping. McKenna wants a tutu, and books about caterpillars.

People stare at you, whisper. "Creepy clown freaks," they say.

Remind McKenna that she's beautiful. Tell her, "We don't pretend anymore, okay?"

Squeeze her hand. Buy her books. Make a scene.

Fact: Clowns can see more spectrums of light than you can. They are not **afraid** of the dark.

Stilts

by Line Henriksen

There's something outside my window.

For a long time it's been banging and rumbling down the street, back and forth, back and forth.

The streetlamp swings silently, small autumn winds twirling it around their fingers as they push past the wires that suspend it above the asphalt deep below. It makes tall shadows dance and leap across my ceiling; they are on the walls, kicking their long legs high, high, impossibly high, almost hitting their heads. They jump and fall, disappearing and reappearing in the frame of my window to the music of the rushing wind. I see the shadows of leaves and plastic bags, caught in the maelstrom, whipping past, chased by—

They stop outside my window.

I live on the fourth floor, but they stop right outside my window.

I close my eyes as the knocking begins.

"Don't you ever worry that something might come for you? From these websites you go to?"

"I go there anonymously. It's really quite safe. Safer than the surface web, anyway."

"And this is the deep one? The deep parts? All full of sharks and whatnot?"

"Nah, that's just what people like to think. That it's some kind of void full of everything from assassins and hackers and drug-dealers to ghosts and monsters and super AIs that speak quantum physics. Those are mostly just urban legends. Really, the Deep Web is primarily boring stuff that hasn't been indexed by search engines yet. Or sensitive information, like personal data from social media and such."

"So when I go on Facebook, I go to the Deep Web?"

"Not really. A bit. It's sort of all over the place, I think. It's not that contained."

"You know, I've been thinking about what you said last time. About being afraid of clowns."

"Can we not?"

There's something outside my window.

It's running down the street, back and forth, back and forth, the sound of wood against asphalt jumping between buildings. The streetlamp twitches, and I see the shadows kick their legs, disappearing and reappearing, jumping and twirling, jumping and twirling, faster and faster; faster and faster. I see them open their mouths wide, deeper and wider, in grins that swallow the shadows of plastic bags and lost leaves.

Until they snap them shut.

Until they stop and they turn and I know they're right above me, their shadows filtering through the curtains like ink, bloating the fabric, growing in size, stretching across my face and my blanket, hitting the floor without a sound and reaching towards the door in the naked wall across the bed.

I hear the knocking and I think *don't look, don't look, don't look...*

"I looked it up on Wikipedia—"

"Oh, come on."

"No, just listen. According to Wikipedia, the word for the fear of clowns — I can't remember what it is right now, something Greek-ish with a C — but, that word, that specific word, it dates back to the 80s but wasn't that popular until the internet. It's a web thing, so... it suits you, I guess..."

"Like I said, can we not?"

"You know what the word means?"

"The word you can't even remember?"

"You're gonna like this, I swear..."

There's something.

There's something.

It knocks on the window, right above my head.

I live on the fourth floor, but it's knocking on the window.

It's right above my head, its shadow on the door.

"The ancient Greeks didn't know clowns as funny things, if there's ever been a funny clown. They just used the word to refer to—"

"To what?"

"Stilt-walkers! I like it, I really do. These things are children of the web, right? I mean, almost. And they wear stilts. Careful they're not coming to get you from out of the depths, huh?"

"Don't."

"Just saying. Stilts."

The knocking has stopped.

I tell myself *don't look, don't look, don't look*, but as the shadows fall across the door, I look. I live on the fourth floor, but the shadows fall through my window and across the door.

The knocking has stopped. The wind has stopped. The streetlamp is still.

The shadows turn the handle, and as the door opens I see—

Nothing. Nothing at all. Just the deep dark of the void, framed by the open door. It seems like I'm no longer lying down, but floating directly above it, watching the darkness unfold. And I wait, and they wait, and we all wait as something gets ready to try on its legs.

Fact: No one has ever seen a clown **blink**.

Fact:
In 1873,
Sir Charles
Hurston
set out to
circumnavigate
the world
in a
clown-skin
balloon.

He crashed
& **burned.**

The balloon
did not.

A Million Tiny Ropes
by Virginia M. Mohlere

What if they let go of the net, JennyAnne thought as she swung in the spot-lit layer of warmth between the dark of the tent peak above and the dark of the floor below. Bert, Robert, and Bobby, practically interchangeable in costume or out of it, a trio of dark heads outside the canteen trailer and a trio of squashed mud-colored fedoras under her every night.

They leaned back from the net's edges and kicked up their oversize shoes until the crowd laughed. They danced back and forth across the ring until the crowd shouted with worry. But the center of the net was always precisely underneath her, no matter how fast or slowly she swung. Always the very center, and their six hands grasping the edges.

"We'll always catch you, JennyAnne," Bert said to her through the window of the women's trailer, while she was peeling off her costume for the night. She snapped the window shade shut over his face.

None of them ever seemed to get all the black liner washed off from around their eyes.

"We'll always catch you, JennyAnne," Robert said, standing behind her at the canteen. She bumped forward into Sheila, the Wolf Lady.

Their breath was always cold on her skin when they stood too close to her and spoke.

"Watch it, darlin'," Sheila said, but pulled JennyAnne into a furry embrace, "you come up here and fill that plate. Get much thinner and you'll take off from that trapeze, fly up off into the night."

Oh, she would, too. Fly up through the hole at the top of the tent and off into the warm summer air, away from nets and clowns and debts and wooden bars chewing up the palms of her hands.

But until that happened, the calluses, the net, and the Roberts were the price she paid for those instants of flight. She slept on the platform sometimes, when they did a double show. High off the ground, safe as a bird in a nest.

JennyAnne sat tucked up between Sheila and Mikhail the Magnificent (Mike Petru from La Grange, Texas) and let them dump extra food on her plate while she pretended not to look. Baked beans, stewed apples, slices of pork roast, and slaw. She let the food sit in her and warm her up, even though it made her heavy, heavy as a thing that might get caught in a net.

You want the net to be taut — just enough to break a fall. But a net has to be a little loose, as well, or a body will bounce up, out, and splatter like an old tomato on the ground right in front of the audience. There are two middle points, one good and one bad.

The good net is the one that's firm but yielding, like a mother teaching manners to a small child. It catches you, keeps you from breaking, with just enough give to hold you close.

The bad net is the one a little too loose. It's the net of getting into cars with the wrong boys. You fall into it, and you go farther than you meant. An extra drop that sends your stomach up into your throat.

Then it folds around you, all those tiny ropes tying you up at once, and you're caught.

Three times, her hand has slipped on the bar while she stares down at the net, trying to judge whether it's a good net or a bad one. Or even a net that will be there at all.

"We'll always catch you, JennyAnne," Bobby had said, in the dark moment before she climbed the ladder to her platform.

His hand on her arm had been like sandpaper. It left a tender spot when she shrugged away.

Her hand had slipped, and when she had glanced down, the six eyes staring up at her were black, glittering. Chips of obsidian under fedoras, above red-painted smiles. For the briefest instant, the lips underneath all that paint also smiled, parted in welcome.

It was stone fear that gave JennyAnne the strength to hang on single-handed, swing her left hand back into place on the bar. She tried yet again to swing herself so high she'd take off, but she always came back down to ground. To the dirt, the power of gravity, and the Roberts, with their permanently shadowed eyes and too-red lips, cold breath and skin like sharks. Circling, with a net.

Fact: The Clown Rebellion of 1623 never ended.
It went underground. The clowns are still waiting.
They are **always** waiting.

Queen and Fool

by Dayle A. Dermatis

Arlecchino. Funny, sad Harlequin. Trapped in the never-ending cycle of wooing Columbina but never having her. The audience laughs.

The truth runs deeper. So does the suffering.

You may never have Columbina, but she has you. Imprisoned, weeping clear tears. You can never find release because the cage doesn't allow you to grow. Lust brings frustration, with a color as red as the crimson diamonds on your costume.

Your mask, with its ridiculously long nose — Columbina designed it. You've worn it so long, it's an extension of you. When she strokes it, the audience laughs at the bawdy entendre. They think you laugh, too, but soundless crying is too easily mistaken for laughter. Because when she strokes it, you imagine that caress elsewhere — you *feel* it elsewhere, but that place can never grow long like your mask's nose.

You ache for her. You throb. You weep.

You're known for your exaggerated gait, your ridiculous wide steps. Only you and Columbina know you move that way because the cage chafes, a constant reminder of your helplessness. Open your legs wide for the cartwheel, Arlecchino. Flip around the stage as if you are free.

You are never free.

They say the beginnings of your story are rooted in hell — that you were a demon serving at the devil's bidding.

The truth is simply this: You are in a hell of your own making. The hell of love, and lust, of hopeless adoration and a deprivation so frustrating you cannot think, only feel, only pray for surcease.

If there is a devil, it is Columbina — but Columbina is your possessor, your heart, your very air. Your angel of anguish.

At night there is no rest for you, because Columbina comes. You give her pleasure with your mouth and hands, tasting her sweet nectar, her thick scent filling your senses. Behind your mask, your eyes plead for mercy, for release.

Unstrap this monstrous cage from me, you beg without words. *Touch me, just once. Once is all it will take...*

Oh, she does touch you, but while you are trapped, the caresses and whispers of hot breath bring no pleasure, only greater punishment. Tears leak from behind your mask even as they leak through the cage as you writhe.

You know if you speak, she will treat your words the same way the audience does, as jests and japes to bring amusement.

That is the one spark of hope left to you: that you bring your beloved Columbina amusement, and pleasure. She could never do the things she does to you if you did not love her so, worship her so. Your denial of pleasure is *her* pleasure, which somehow brings it back to being *your* pleasure.

It makes no sense, but then, isn't your role, your very being, nonsensical?

Columbina will always be the queen, and you will always be the fool.

Funny, sad, tormented Arlecchino.

Fact: Clowns lack **blood** and plasma.
However, they are the Red Cross's
most **generous** donors. If you need,
they will find you **vital** fluids.

God's Children

by Jason Arias

Jinx is lacing up his 96-eye, combat clown-er boots on the edge of his bed. No frame, no box spring, just a mattress. The WWJD fitted sheet is un-cornered at the top side of the mattress, revealing the irregular borders of a yellow under-staining. It's too high up to be a piss stain. Well, hell, I guess it could be.

Jinx hasn't been himself of late; been drinking himself upside-down. That isn't quite a sin in DOHL doctrine, but his uncleanliness pushes up against subtle transgression. The red afro wig Jinx is wearing is peppered in lint and torn paper products. He'd lost his wig fashioned of real hair, didn't say how. What he's wearing now looks stolen from The Party Store.

Jinx looks like a goddamn kid, with his head between his parachute pants-ed knees, fumbling with his laces. He's not even wearing his *biggie* hands and he's acting all *clambidextrous* — the term used for a seemingly clumsy, but calculated, misdirection — but I don't think he's acting.

71

"Need some help with that?"

"No," he says, all snotty like.

"Fix the corner of your bed," I say and kick the edge of the mattress. The fitted sheet pops out of a second spot.

"Watcha do that for, Sub?"

I hadn't meant to pop that second corner, but I let him think it purposeful anyway.

"Watcha livin' like this for, brother?" I say.

Jinx ain't my biological kin, but we're brothers in the clown-i-logical sense.

"Come on, Sub, go easy," he says. My name's short for Subliminal. I was given it by DOHL — pronounced like the pineapple brand, extrapolated into: Devotees Of a Higher Laughter — upon initial assignment to the Propaganda Division. The work wasn't hard. You grow up with six drunken uncles and you hear a lot of tale-spinning.

"If the other brothers saw you, you think they'd say less?" I ask.

Jinx was my academy-mate — both of us moved up to Operatives at the same time — which means it's up to me to call him on his shit, remind him why we face-powder up, remind him that God laughs with us as long as we keep serving him, but can turn his back on us just as easy.

Believe me, there's a God up there and he's concerned, but not about whether you have wi-fi in the shower, or if little Janey goes to boarding school or not. He sees your pettiness and laughs his ass off at it. My fellow DOHL brothers and sisters are laughing right along with him. I'm laughing with him. Maybe we're juggling your kitchen knives, in the living room, when you get home. Maybe we're trying on your wife's makeup to enhance our two-inch thick red lip borders before kissing the glass door of the shower you're in. Maybe you don't find the humor in this.

I was you once, but have become more.

That WWJD sheet that keeps coming off Jinx's mattress is a trophy straight from the twin bed of the first child we ever turned into a message, together. It ain't easy. The messages ain't personal, certainly not sexual, not like the newspapers portray — there's a special palm-buzzer placement in Hell for that particular proclivity. We only did to the child what was needed. Didn't mess with his head none, took him real quick. Left him like a Jehovah's Witness leaflet for his parents to find on the doorstep; all folded up and silent.

He's laughing with God now for his martyrdom.

You think it ain't right, doncha?

Well, just like God, I'm laughing atcha. You want to make people more present, you take away their future. Start martyring their children and they pay attention.

Hell, this ain't nothing new. Don't you watch the news? They make little boys into bombs elsewhere.

Jinx is done tying his laces, but he still looks like shit. His giant polka dot bowtie is undone all scarf-like. Like some Hugh Grant clown-i-tion. Some Oscar Wilderness care-not Englishman. Jinx's parachute pants have mustard, and what looks like ketchup globs, all up and down them. Even the W-COHC (Wayward Clan Of Hobo Clowns) looks more put together than he is.

"Jinx," I say, shaking my head, "you got to get it together."

There's a quick scuffling sound from Jinx's closet, behind him. Probably rats making a nest with rolled-away nose balls. Jinx's head twitches in the direction of the sound, like he's afraid I'm gonna say something about the correlation of uncleanliness and varmints.

He rolls quick onto his belly, on the mattress, and starts fussing with corner of the WWJD sheet there, trying to run an impromptu skit, like he can't hook the corner right, trying to generate some divine laughter from me. But I'm not feeling Godly right now. I'm just feeling disgusted. I always wondered why Jinx had to take that *trophy* in the first place — the sheet that belonged to that first child. Didn't sit right with me. Martyrs don't need their left-behinds stolen.

Plus, we're Operatives. We shouldn't be taking our work home with us. It ain't healthy.

There's a louder scuffling from the closet area and a definite thump too big to be a rat. Jinx faux-falls off the mattress and pretend-brains himself on the hardwood, but it's a poorly timed cover-up. He throws himself into a clown-tantrum. All dramat-i-cals.

I step around his kicking legs, make my way to the closet back there.

"No," Jinx says reaching out with one hand from the floor.

"What's in here, Jinx?"

"Please, Sub."

I turn the handle and open the closet door. I see him straight away. The should've-been martyr from last week that Jinx said he'd take care of alone, but clearly didn't. The boy's naked from the chest up. Looks like Jinx has been cutting slow on him. There's duct tape on his wrists, and legs, and mouth.

It'll be two messages we send tonight, this one and the one we've just been assigned. I haven't figured what to do with Jinx yet. I can't find the laughter in me right now.

I'm sorry Jinx toyed with this martyr; God don't require that.

I'll set him free though.

He'll be laughing eternal before long.

Fact: When you laugh, a clown laughs with you.
When you **cry**, the clown laughs harder.

Fact: Clowns can switch off their sense of **pain** when they **crush** their bodies into cars by the hundreds. But they don't.

Clown's Syndrome

by Joe Nazare

"Think Ripley's more than Ringling," Nestor tells his carload. "Dare-I-believe-my-eyes kind of spectacle."

Most of his fellow travelers have already formed audience to this story over the past few days. They ride along quiescently now as Nestor recounts for his latest passenger, picked up tonight outside a Macy's in Joliet.

"Not that anyone who came to see Val Kearny's Bizarro Side-show wasn't expecting the incredible. And Val gave it to 'em in spades: the Bee-Bearded Lady, the Lobster Boy Knife-Thrower, the Illustrated Woman Hootchie-Kootch. Where else would you find a trapeze act conducted above an electrified 'safety' net? Even that seemed hardly death-defying compared to the risks Ziggy and Lloyd took every night as our Lion Shamers."

The blackened sky and lack of traffic along this stretch of I-80 makes the surrounding scene appear even more boundless, but retrospection serves to restrict Nestor's purview. "Naturally I'm biased," he admits, "but for me the clown-car routine was the epitome of the Sideshow's twisted vision. We weren't rehashing 'that antiquated antic,' as Val's spiel assured. No canned fanfare, no exaggeratedly clumsy exits.

No floppy shoes or baggy outfits. Necessity streamlined our costumes — just skinsuits and greasepainted faces." Afterwards, each smeared performer resembled Heath Ledger following a hard day battling the Dark Knight.

"We'd start out queued up, a bright, numbered balloon pictured on each of our chests like a coat of arms. Val's proclamation of 'Send in the clowns!' was our signal to fall in: one by one we'd sprawl headfirst through the driver's side window-space. That interior got cramped damned quick, and then every new addition would force us to turn contortionist. With all fifty of us stuffed inside, we made Siamese twins look like distant relatives. I'm talking total mob scene." Yet the antithesis of unruliness. Their mass of bodies was sublimely interwoven, like something out of a Clive Barker story. An intricate meshwork of flesh that—

A rapid double thud preempts reverie, as Nestor steers straight across a moon-crater of a pothole, jolting everybody in the vehicle. Nestor immediately bounces a look off the rearview mirror. "Sorry, guys," he offers, as the rattled resettle.

"Now I don't doubt," Nestor resumes his narrative, "that plenty of viewers found our writhing oddly erotic, and yeah, certain clowns would seek even tighter fits with each other after the show. For me, though, it was always more about the camaraderie, the choreography. I loved the midmorning rehearsals just as much as the nightly performances. Loved the *discipline* our confinement required." Fingernails and waistlines alike needed to be kept courteously trim. Strong mouthwash and deodorant was mandatory, flatulence a carnival sin.

"Our act changed names periodically, but maintained the theme: the Sardine Sedan, the Cooped DeVille. It was after Val christened it the Claustrophobile during our Oklahoma circuit that I suggested installing the dash cams. And lemme tell you, once we started flashing our restricted gymnastics up on a big screen, there was just as much squirming going on out in the audience. From there, Val came up with the 'jester ejector' wrinkle. He'd draw a numbered clown-nose from a hopper, and we'd have to work to somehow crowd-surf the corresponding body out the window. Val was always plotting, always trying to push the proverbial envelope. Hmmph, one time, the crazy bastard floated the idea of setting the car in the middle of *a demolition derby*."

Nestor grows quiet, his smile flatlining. "Fortunately or not, we never gave that one a test-drive," he says at last. "Because for reasons only he'll ever know, Val decided to see how many Lunesta could fit inside a man's stomach." The boss took the big sleep inside his trailer, and overnight the Bizarro Sideshow was no more.

Stunned, Nestor returned to Jersey, not because he had any family left there; he just didn't know where else to go. He spent the next nineteen months mostly moping around his apartment, living off unemployment checks and his meager savings, having no desire to launch a new job search. Deep down, there was only one type of labor he ached to perform, and the local want ads wouldn't be listing it. But then, unexpected as a brain attack, inspiration struck last Sunday night as he sat half-watching *The Walking Dead*: the idea for an extraordinary variation on the Claustrophobile. A perfect venue, too, sprang to mind.

Revitalized, he worked the phone feverishly, but his disbanded Sideshow brothers proved unreachable or uninterested. Nestor, though, was undeterred, and resolved to hit the road. He'd simply recruit as he cruised cross-country.

"Sin City isn't gonna know what hit it!" Nestor enthuses, delighted to have gathered the makings of a new troupe. It might be easy to dismiss a single person pitching such an outré idea as the Meat Waggin, but a whole posse of ready demonstrators could be amazingly persuasive. What casino wouldn't hire them on after seeing how they would pack themselves in?

Excited as he is by the prospect, Nestor suddenly wants nothing more than to stop driving. When he sees the roadside pictograph promising lodging up ahead, he proposes a rest-of-the-night respite. No one protests, so he takes the next exit and pulls into the motel parking lot. He selects and backs into a spot in the corner farthest from the building.

Nestor kills the engine, gets out and steps around back of the car. "Another day closer to Vegas," he cheerily announces to the occupants as he pops open the trunk.

Travel has taken obvious toll on Nestor's enlistees, whose disfigured forms litter the compartment. Severed limbs have rolled away from unclothed torsos. Decapitated heads lie scattered, cueball-bald, their respective faces smooth blanks save for nose-suggesting bumps.

Nestor's nape begins to itch as he senses the immense emptiness of the cosmos looming overhead. Averting his gaze from the jumble of pallid plastic parts before him, Nestor casts a surreptitious look around the parking lot. Satisfied, he plants one foot on the Taurus's bumper, directly above the Garden State license plate that reads MYSP88. A second later, he's climbing inside, and pulling the trunk a sliver short of shut. Settling down within the luxurious heap, he proceeds to brush up on the old act with his newest, closest friends.

FACT: Clowns have no **lines** on their palms.
If you want to tell a clown's fortune
you must **read** its elbows.

Fact: Clowns make their own make-up. Red from **ochre**,
black from charcoal, and white from the
bleached **bones** of bodies they once inhabited

Clown Car, Driven Once, Never Emptied

by Karlo Yeager-Rodriguez

The fucking salesman promised the car was clean.

Dan's knuckles creaked as he gripped the steering wheel like it was his salvation, eyes on shifting traffic on the rain-soaked highway. He heard them all around him, furtive movements in the hidden spaces of the car: the rustle as they moved under the back seat, the stifled titters echoing from inside the glove box, the squeak of red plastic noses crushed against each other.

The car was still full of them.

Dan kept his eyes fixed on the lane ahead, squinting past the steady swish of the wipers to the snarl of fast-moving cars on the expressway. No sirens, no flashing lights in the rearview, good.

Back at the dealership, the salesman had oozed up to Dan, who stared at the jaundice-yellow VW Bug. "I can see you're a collector," he'd crooned and nodded at the horrid little lump of a car contained by the circle of velvet ropes.

Like one of those magic circles, Dan had thought.

"It's from that show." Dan had gulped. "Uncle Hasty's?"

"Sure," the salesman nodded, and his smile grew stale as his eyes flicked between the Bug and Dan. "A good price, too." Dan nodded, and looked back across the street, where the police cars' blue and red lights flashed like a ballyhoo over the arch, the arcade, the big top. He needed to make a getaway.

Aversion therapy. Dan had shuddered at the thought.

On the highway, a shadow fell over the car.

An 18-wheeler breached the waters of the downpour and loomed over him like a wall. Dan slammed on the brakes, palm crushed against the horn. He panted, legs trembling, and jerked his hand off the horn. Its bleating trailed off into nothing like a deflating balloon.

Faded letters framed a big top on the truck container's doors. Dan wiped at the fogged glass to peer through the rain. A smiling clown loomed over the cartoon tent like a bloated, hungry moon.

Dan hurled himself backwards against his seat with a cry. He threw his arms up to cover his face and lifted his feet off the pedals. The car lurched forward, shuddered and drifted — its motor dead.

The rustling became louder.

"You're not listening," his little girl had said, raising her voice over the laughter of the crowd around them. Dan could not believe Emily liked the circus, but there he was, watching a clown car loop around one of the three rings.

"Hm," Dan said. "What's that, Em?" His eyes followed the clown car zippping over the packed dirt, wary as someone watching a large spider scurry across the floor.

"What's going on between you and mom?" Emily craned her head to look over his shoulder, past the stands where her mother had gone to find the restrooms.

Dan glanced at the clown car as its doors popped open.

"We — I, that is," Dan stammered. "I need to go away."

"Why?" Emily's face scrunched up. "For how long?"

Dan shook his head and thought of what he could say, but his eyes were drawn to the clowns tumbling out of the car. The ring will hold them, he had mumbled. They can't cross.

The glove box door popped open with a giggle.

Coasting behind the semi, Dan leaned across, eyes squeezed shut. He slapped the glove box door closed with a whimper. He snapped his eyes open as he heard the back seat thud into place. His gaze darted to the rear view mirror.

Was the tip of an oversized red shoe sticking out like a tongue between black vinyl lips? The giggles grew into crazed shrieks before Dan remembered what could happen if the car stopped without a circle to contain them.

He turned the key and pumped the gas pedal until the engine chirruped to life. He jammed the car into gear, and turned to accelerate past the 18-wheeler. The sounds, the movement stopped. He flipped the painted clown face the finger as he moved past, caught in the flow of traffic again.

"Why," Em repeated. "Why?"

Dan had wanted to explain how after he'd been abandoned as a kid it chipped away at him, how his wife could no longer love his brokenness.

"I don't know, honey," he said and squeezed her hand.

He'd read the reports about the day his momma disappeared, and left him strapped in his high chair in front of the TV, the awful Clown in Yellow show playing. The neighbors found him, hours later, in a soiled diaper, shrieking and pointing at the TV. None of reports explained what he saw: his momma transformed into a cartoon clown on TV, the Clown in Yellow turning and smiling at Dan through the screen.

What could he have told Em — he was cursed?

Haunted by clowns?

He had opened his mouth, teetered on the edge of confession, when he had felt a hand on his shoulder.

A white gloved hand.

He whirled with a shriek and pounded his fists into the chalk-white face again and again until, panting, he'd found teeth embedded in his greasepaint and blood covered knuckles.

Dan felt his blood drain as he'd looked at the mime sprawled at his feet, at the row of clowns, lined along the edge of the ring, looking at him and smiling. He had shrunk before his wife's and Em's open-mouthed horror and fled.

He popped the clutch and felt a gloved hand brush his ankle. His throat clenched around a shriek.

There was a clown hidden under his seat!

A shiver crawled up his leg and up his back, grew into a shudder. The minute he stopped, unbound, they would tumble out of their hidey-holes in the car and out into the world in wave after wave.

He couldn't inflict this horror on the rest of the world. Dan revved the motor. The world would not fall under an endless stream of painted, leering faces and oceans of seltzer water.

The low titters of the hidden clowns sounded quizzical, as he drifted across three lanes of traffic.

✻

Fact: Since 1953, Detroit has been **forced** to
build a clown into every car.
We recommend you take **mass** transit.

Fact: The average human heart rate is 60-100 beats per minute. A clown's is 10-30. You won't hear the difference till you're far too **close**.

Perfect Mime

by Sara K. McNeilly

She wears her makeup to bed each night. It sloughs off with the dead skin cells and clogs the pillowcase. It gets thick and stiff with pastel oil. The mornings are routine scrapings. With a straight edge barber's razor she shaves her face back into a tin and melts it into place. Each day wears greyer, thinner, and less complete.

She starts her day with a ritual. Lights fire to dark pencils and marks herself for sacrifice. Thick dark lines stroke on a grey white surface. She puts her features back in place. Feels for the indents and ridges on her canvas and draws the template of a face. Stipples in irises and pupils. Fills in lips and brows. Brushes on shadow and light.

Each morning ends with Walter's knock at the door. Hand smacks on the vanity table. He opens. He enters. She waits.

"Good morning," he says. He touches her elbow and brings her to her feet. His fingers press into her jaw and hold her face in the warm light of the lamp. Walter's tongue clucks against his teeth. "Still not right, doll. The features are there but you need to put the costume makeup on too." He drags a cold damp pencil down her cheek and pulls it in an upward stroke. He does the same to the other side. Black diamonds dripping in long points down her face.

"Perfect," he mutters. He opens the closet door and asks "Which today, doll? Stripes? No, no. Not Stripes. Motley, I think." He speaks as if to an empty room. Walter dresses her with a practised deftness. He spins her in a circle, like a gentleman does his lady, and he leads her out the door.

She begins her evenings in a slow waltz. Spins in time without a partner and stares without seeing into the laughing crowd. Bows. Dips. Floats like a ballerina, and taps out rhythms with precision.

The room fills as she moves. People take their places on the benches. Tickets slide into back pockets. Popcorn flows over bags, hands, mouths. Spills on the floor. Hands cover mouths. They clap together. They clasp in excitement.

When her partner joins, they are flawless. He hisses each move. She tries to escape. Hits invisible walls. Perfectly timed. She slides to the floor. Palms press flat against nothing. Fingers curl and scratch down the air. She slaps the walls. Silent.

The audience cheers. They whistle spittle and cotton candy. Blue drool glaze slick on tongues. They clap. They laugh. Their glee is clear. Electric. Cracking between their lips.

Her partner reaches through the wall and hauls her up by the fringe of her blue and black motley neck. He holds her close and bends his mouth to her ear. He steps away and pulls a length of unseen rope from a bottomless pocket. Her arms lift in time up over her head. Bending limp at the wrist. The man in matching motley circles her. He smiles at the cheering audience. He drinks their joy. He pulls off an imagined belt. He folds it. He snaps it taut. She flinches in time with the noiseless contact of air on air. Head tilts away from the man.

He steps behind her and brings his hand down in a sweeping arc. She pulls the imagined restraints tight.

Arches away from the whip. Stands on the ends of her toes. Bends like a bow.

He whips her again and again.

He whips her until she slumps in the air.

He whips her until the audience stills.

Silent when he cuts the left tether.

Silent when he cuts the right.

Silent when her body hits the floor.

He pulls her to her feet and holds her like a giant rag doll. Twists in a tango turn.

They cheer.

The man bends his mouth again. She backs away. Her hand covers her face. Cheekbone to jaw. She runs like prey. Runs until she doesn't. Runs until she hits another wall. Drops to her knees.

Her partner turns to the audience and bows with a wink. He pulls another length of rope from his pocket. He ties it in a loop and spins it around himself. He hops over it. Legs kick on high. A cartoon cowboy for the glutted crowd.

He swings the invisible rope over his head with one hand and flings it around her neck. Her fingers rush to her throat and tug at it. She crawls towards him. He pulls the rope tight. Hand over fist, he pulls her steadily. He pauses. Winks at the audience once more. Jerks at the rope. She falls forward on the floor. Hands caught under her body. Elbows cracking on the floor.

He pulls.

Gasps from the audience are louder than the squeak of skin on polished wood. He lifts the rope and her body follows. Scrambles. Feet kick out from underneath her. Fingers scratch at the invisible cord around her neck. He pulls her level. Wraps an arm around her waist. Tips her back. Dips deep. Lifts. Carries her bridal style out of the tent. He trips over the length of rope that hangs from her neck. He turns and bows.

And he runs away.

The audience loves it.

Her evenings begin the same way each night. Lays flat on her stomach and Walter wipes a cold cloth soaked in rubbing alcohol along her ripped and welted back.

"Flawless performance tonight, doll," Walter coos at her. "Inspired."

Walter picks up a picture of her as a little girl from the nightstand. Pulls a pencil from the inside pocket of his coat. Runs the pink tip of the eraser over her mouth and eyes. Burns them away into the whiteness of the paper. Removes them. Draws smooth skin in place.

Walter lays her down on her mattress. He lays her face down on her pillow. He strokes her hair. He whispers his goodnight into a kiss at the back of her head. He walks out the door and locks it behind him.

She falls asleep the same way each night. Face presses into the mattress. Her made up face rubs off into the pillowcase.

Walter's voice rings in her ears.

"The perfect mime."

Fact: Clowns can remove their **bones** at will.
That's how they fit so many in cars,
and how they **slip** under your door.

Fact: Clowns are naturally buoyant.
We **do not** recommend using them as
flotation devices in case of emergency.

Whaling with Clowns
by Chris Kuriata

"Whale!"

Being the only seaman still strong enough to climb the decaying rigging to the top of the whaleship *Jungfrau*, Starbuck drew crow's nest duty.

"There she blows! — There she blows!"

Captain Alloway stumbled from his cabin, wearing only sleeping britches and boots, the soles of which had been boiled and eaten weeks ago. He lifted a spyglass to his eye and saw the gorgeous hump of a sperm whale breaching. For three excruciating months, the ship's hold remained empty, yet Captain Alloway stubbornly stayed to course, ignoring all evidence he had sailed into dead waters, where not even the fabled tentacle-beasts lurked in the polluted blackness. The long awaited appearance of a whale meant the *Jungfrau* would not perish.

"Ready the clown!" Alloway commanded his crew. "Bring me Sew-Toes the Clown!"

Starbuck scrambled from the crow's nest, barreling down the narrow passage to Sew-Toes' cell. The walls were still stained with the blood of Stubbs, Sew-Toes' previous handler. The whaler peered through iron bars at the dozing clown; both the most dangerous being on the ocean and the *Jungfrau's* only chance for survival.

The chains wrapped around Sew-Toes' chest were broken, the sturdy links dissolved by his acidic drool. Starbuck feared the clown tearing through his restraints as easily as dry cornsilk. Ignoring the bone chilling growl of Sew-Toes' empty belly, Starbuck used his harpoon to open the door and prod the weary clown.

Sew-Toes' nostrils swelled to the size of bass mouths, inhaling the fresh sea air. His coiled eyes stared through Starbuck. Sew-Toes smelled the whale; the sperm oil in the leviathan's head sang to him like rum to a drunkard.

With his harpoon plunged deep into Sew-Toes' ribcage, Starbuck manoeuvred the clown out of the hold into daylight. Clowns need circus canvas for protection from the painful rays of the sun. Oozing boils sprouted beneath Sew-Toes' pancaked face. The distraction worked to Starbuck's favour, making Sew-Toes easier to load aboard the smaller whaleboat lowering over the side of the *Jungfrau*.

Six oarsmen to each side pulled the boat across the trembling sea. White froth broke over their skeletal arms. Sew-Toes stood with one foot on the tip of the bow, his red nose pointing the way, following the rich scent of sperm oil. Sew-Toes flapped his gums, whinnying like a horse, as clowns often did when teased with the scent of whales.

Once the boats reached the breaching whale, Alloway gave the order.

"Remove the chains!"

Before his bonds were fully stripped, Sew-Toes dived gracefully into the ocean. One of the rowers, Pip, snagged his wrist in the trailing chains and was lifted right out of his boots, disappearing into the deep waters behind the clown. No one wasted a second looking for Pip to resurface. They all knew he wouldn't.

Captain Alloway pulled a pipe from his vest and rested comfortably. "Now, we wait."

While clowns have been used since the earliest days of whaling, no man knows for certain how a clown singlehandedly slaughters a whale. When the enormous beasts float belly up to the surface, their bodies never reveal injury. The whales die pristine, beatific even, like Saints. The body of a whale killed by a clown does not decay, no matter how long you leave it hoisted astern. The nautical museum at New Bedford displays a sperm whale killed by Moosecorn the Clown in 1873. Fifteen years later, the specimen has yet to show the slightest hint of decomposition.

Veteran seamen have their own idea of how clowns slay a whale. One popular theory holds that clowns crawl through a whale's tailpipe and twist their intestines into knotted sculptures; dogs and horses and the like. Another is that clowns employ sleight-of-hand to show the whale a magic trick which causes the mammal's ignorant brain to doubt natural laws and die of shock. Another theory claims clowns understand the enigma of whale humour and tell the whale a joke so funny the great beast dies laughing.

Academics roll their eyes at these theories, insisting clowns merely put whales into "an intense state of hibernation" using acupressure, but no one listens to these beard-stroking book-heads, who've never set foot on a whaling vessel their entire lives.

Captain Alloway packed a second pipe while the men waited, dreaming already of whale steaks nourishing them back to vitality. Had the seamen not been so desperate, they would have recognized something was wrong and rowed quickly back to the *Jungfrau*. They might have made it.

Just as the whalers of yore wouldn't bring a dull harpoon to slay a whale, seamen knew never to send a starving clown into the ocean. The horror stories were well known, but the crew of the *Jungfrau* had taken the risk. Under the circumstances, what other choice did they have?

Blood began to warm the waters surrounding the boat. A well-fed clown could always be trusted to send a slaughtered whale to the surface unscratched, but Sew-Toes ripped into the whale's main pipeline, flooding the ocean, turning the sea the color of borscht. He did this not to satiate his hunger. He longed to hunt a different type of sea-life.

Captain Alloway remained stoic. He packed the last of his surrogate tobacco (wood shavings chiselled off the deck of the *Jungfrau*) into his pipe. He got two puffs before Sew-Toes rammed the bottom of the whaleboat, propelled by his bulbous feet through the water with the speed of a cannon ball.

The boat shattered into matchstick splinters, dropping injured men into the churning, red froth. Some cried repentance of their sins. The smarter ones opened their throats for the sea to flood, hoping to drown before Sew-Toes found hold of them. No one escaped, not even Captain Alloway, who had purchased Sew-Toes as an infant from a roving band of clowns in Bremen four score years ago.

One by one, the *Jungfrau's* seamen learned the mystery behind how a clown killed a whale without leaving a mark. "Funny that," Starbuck managed to think through his agony, "It seems so obvious once you know."

Fact: Fingernails are a **delicacy** for clowns.
The fact that they grow so slowly on human hands
just makes them more **coveted**.

Fact: Extensive testing has **proven**
that clowns are fire-resistant.
The scientists who carried out the tests were not.

Clown Shoes

by Cassandra Khaw

I told him not to look. I told him. But Jameson's always had a gluttonous curiosity. The kind that chews and chews on your liver until you give it what it wants.

He didn't just glance at the thing when we passed by the enclosure. He really *looked*. Just straight-up gawked like the idiot he was.

"He doesn't have shoes," he said in his little-boy voice.

Of course not, I said. Discarded clowns don't get to have shoes. Everyone knows that. Except for Jameson, of course, but he really should have known better. He was twelve. Twelve is too old to be naive about clowns.

"But he looks so sad."

It, I reminded him. Not he. And of course it does, I said. Clowns are tied to their shoes. The same way selkies are bound to their skins and bird-wives are chained to their feathers. That's how the world works.

"What does it look like with its shoes on, then?"

Ask mom, I hissed as I dragged him out of the slaughter-red tent. Jameson shut up immediately, like my order was a slap. He was just a baby — lucky brat — when the clowns came for dad, but he heard the stories.

The drive home was caked in uneasy silence. Fog crawled up through the Oregonian undergrowth to take bites out of the fat white moon. From time to time, Jameson would point out eyes in the bushes. Feral clowns. Officially, they weren't any more dangerous than your average grizzly. But I still didn't like them.

"I don't like red," Jameson said as we closed in on the edge of our town, which glowed like a wound in the night.

You'd like it a whole lot more if you were being chased by a clown, I said, as I rolled my eyes and fiddled with the rear-view mirror. Clowns aren't afraid of anything but red, I add, savage. It's why they eat with their eyes clamped shut.

A silhouette blurred in the glass: too tall, too thin, too strange to be anything but a clown. My heart seized. It has no shoes, I thought numbly to myself, seconds before it pounced out of sight.

I didn't let off the gas pedal until we got home.

"The clown won't go away."

I nodded sleepily and rubbed more lavender oil into Jameson's temples. The scratching on the door grew louder. As far as clowns went, the one that followed Jameson home wasn't so bad. It mostly just slept under our beds, rolled out like a Persian rug, muscles and cartilage deflated. Sometimes, it would try to eat the family cat, but that wasn't really a problem either. Our Moggie could take care of herself even if the floorboards couldn't.

"I'm sorry," Jameson whimpered.

I spooned my fingers through his hair, tried to ignore the gleam of his pale skin, the powderiness of his scalp. Jameson is immune. We're all immune, thanks to mom's genes. The doctor said so. We're immune to the airborne vector. The doctors *said* so.

"Just a clown," I told him as I nodded again. Kissed his forehead. Jameson clutched at my shirt, his nose ringtop-red, his skin boiling.

The scraping noise grew into a pounding like a giant's heartbeat.

Stupid kid. I told him. I told Jameson not to look. But he did, and now we're haunted by a discarded clown.

"Don't think about it. It's nothing," I repeated. Clowns without their shoes aren't anybody, least of all a dad.

In desperation, I brought my father's loafers to the clown, thinking it would bring us full circle. You break family curses by going back to the sole of the matter, don't you? More importantly, if it had shoes, maybe it'd go away and find somewhere else to haunt. But the clown only sniffed at them and wriggled back under Jameson's bed, copper-coin eyes staring, bright as accusation.

As my little brother began to lose his color, I started offering it other footwear: my sneakers, mom's high heels, Jameson's baby shoes. No luck there either. Catalogs filled with expensive boots and novelty shoes drew only contemptuous snuffles, fashion shows growls of uncertain pleasure. Then, it hit me.

Clowns need clown shoes.

But you can't just buy clown shoes off the shelf. You can't even get them fresh. They wither the moment their host dies. The only time I've seen a clown acquire another clown's shoes was on a documentary when a pack of hatchlings ate their way to the toe-bones of a dying elder. Something about the nourishing intestinal bacteria and symbiotic intraspecies relationships. I don't know. There are a lot of theories about clowns, lots of evidence, all of which contradictory, half of which quarter-way wrong.

I *guess* we could have gone with a feral. But I figured we should maximize our chances for success. Why risk it? Mom volunteered for the role, but I said no. She already tried once. But we lost Dad to Grandpop anyway. Besides, Jameson needs a mom more than he needs a sister who was too chicken to save their father.

If it's any consolation, the doctors said the transformation process is relatively painless; mild fever, aching joints, a loss of voice. Much easier than what Jameson is going through. The shoes release hallucinogenic compounds when they attach themselves to your feet so there's nothing to be worried of there, either.

And yeah, clowns can regrow their shoes, at least those who are nursed on inside jokes, who are kept inside and not in highway museums. It's fine. It'll be fine. Pass me the nose and lock the door on your way out.

Just make sure not to think any funny thoughts in the house for a while, okay? Newborns apparently get a little antsy in the first weeks.

Fact: All clowns have the **same** birthday,
but nobody knows when **it** is.

Fact: There is always at **least** one more clown inside a mirror reflection than there is standing in front of the **mirror**.

A Silent Comedy

by Cate Gardner

The mime reached under the cubicle door and grabbed at Rita's ankles. A black-painted eye and half-a-hideous grin peered beneath the door. She kicked out at his white-gloved-fingers. Her hands caught her scream. Another mime climbed onto the toilet in the neighbouring cubicle and peered down at Rita. She swallowed her scream and shook her head. She wouldn't give them her voice.

She wouldn't. She wouldn't. She wouldn't.

Biting her lips tight, Rita dug into her handbag for something to tape her lips together, found nothing. As the mime above tried to drop into her cubicle, his fingers crawling through her hair, Rita slapped against him and lost the tip of her scream. The mime grabbing at her feet caught the end of her shriek, swallowing it so it rumbled in his belly. She couldn't stay in here.

Gathering her nerve, Rita stood and dragged at the cubicle door. Her scalp hurt as the mime above stole several strands of hair. She tripped over the outstretched leg of the mime on the floor. Her gasp travelled across the bathroom and the mime above grabbed it in his fist and ate it whole. Rita shook her head. She wouldn't give them anything else. Scrambling for the door, she managed to pull it open. It didn't creak, squeak or even swish for the mimes had already stolen its sounds.

She pulled the door shut and held onto the handle so those trapped inside the bathroom couldn't escape. As a hand tapped her on the shoulder, Rita almost lost more of her cry. A mime offered her a pretend drink. The bar was full of them. Mimes sat at the bar, mimes arm-wrestled each other and played bouncers, others sat amongst the sparse patrons, urging them to give up their conversations.

"Leave me be," a girl shouted, and with that her voice was gone.

What was this place? It had looked like an ordinary bar from the outside. *The Circus* — a red brick building with a blue and yellow awning. Mimes guarded the door.

Rita let go of the bathroom door and made her way to the juke-box. Her fists soundlessly pounded against glass until it cracked. The jukebox offered a last shattering gasp, its songs long gone. Broken glass sliced at her palms. She just needed to find a way out, and then she could scream until it hurt. Bloody fingers slipped against the glass as she grabbed the largest shard. As a mime leant in to steal whatever sounds remained, Rita stabbed upwards and caught it in the neck. Its pain offered no noise, nor did his drop. The other mimes moved back, offering exaggerated shock.

They did not fear her. She wasn't that stupid. Slashing at the air, Rita moved towards the bar door. The bouncers moved aside. She would make it out.

She would. She would. She would.

The door gave way behind her back. The mimes crept forward with exaggerated steps and horrified expressions. Rita drew blood from her lip as she fought to contain the barrage of words that she wanted to scream at this troupe. She had to warn her friends not to come in here. She'd made a mistake. Heel connected with and scratched against pavement. She danced back. Her subsequent steps didn't offer any sound. Rita slammed her heel against the pavement but it didn't even creak. She waved her fists at the bar. The mimes offered a fake-laugh. She would thump their smug faces.

You're out, out, out.

Pumping her arms against the air, she turned and stalked off. At the corner of the street, a car rushed through a puddle of water and showered Rita.

"Fucking idiot," she screamed, and then the rest of her words dragged painfully from her throat until there were none left.

The car backed up, the window rolled down, and a mime tipped his ribbon-edged hat and grin, grin, grinned.

FACT: When a clown spontaneously **combusts**
it leaves a pile of tinsel exactly **half** its original mass.

Pushpin and Pullpin
by Charles Payseur

Pushpin and Pullpin were born in their sixteenth year of life. At sixteen they were old for being born, but Master Pinhead always told them, "You weren't born before you were a clown," and that meant they could bend some rules. Before then, who can say? Were they even twins, as they were afterward, born on the same day, in the same minute, of the same clown that blessed them and bid them rise anew? Whatever they were before, afterward they were linked.

They complimented each other, did Pushpin and Pullpin, and in their makeup and wigs they looked nearly identical, the only difference a small star painted above Pushpin's left eye.

Pushpin was slower, though, more reserved, and while Pullpin would throw a pie into the face of God, Pushpin would be left to face the Judgment, the Almighty apparently too lazy to remember who had the star and who didn't. Pullpin would open all the animal cages and Pushpin would be mauled. Pullpin would light a fuse, and Pushpin would get a face full of soot and fire. "You gotta laugh," Master Pinhead would tell them, and so Pushpin would laugh, and Pullpin would laugh louder, and the crowds would roar loudest of all, and for a while there it worked.

It was exhausting, though, for Pushpin. To always be rushing after, always taking the hits, always suffering, watching the crowds cheer his smiling agony. To them his screams sounded like delighted squeals, his sobs booming guffaws. "Clowns speak only the language of laughter," Master Pinhead always said. But under the serene surface of the mask of joyous makeup, Pushpin was flailing.

Did a part of him wish that, maybe once, the punishment would fall where it belonged? Did a part of him wonder if maybe the crowds laughed because, in his suffering, they were allowed to think he deserved it, that they didn't, that all was right and good because who wasn't Pullpin, or wanted to be?

So one act, when Pullpin had rigged a chair at the edge of a shark tank, perhaps Pushpin arrived a bit late to demand the spot. To demand that he be allowed to sit on chair legs Pullpin had sawed and weakened. Perhaps he waited a moment longer than he knew was wise. And perhaps he watched as Pullpin tumbled in and the crowd stared, laughless, as the crystal water stained red.

Of course, something else Master Pinhead had always said was "Once a clown, always a clown." So Pushpin shouldn't have been too surprised when death only improved Pullpin's routine. Because a ghost can fit into even the smallest of cars. Can float dozens of pies at a time with spectral energy. And when Pullpin called the strongman a prancing dandy, how the crowd applauded at Pushpin's attempts to explain that a ghost had said it. And even more at the thrashing that followed.

The act flourished. Larger audiences, larger spectacles. Hospital bills mounted. Two months recovering after a donkey fractured Pushpin's femur. Two more from the buckshot after Pullpin had stolen the state flag of Alabama and used it in unspeakable ways. Emergency surgery and detox after Pullpin had replaced whiskey with nail polish remover in Pushpin's flask, and that while they were alone, without even an audience. "A clown is never off-duty," Master Pinhead had taught them. And who was Pushpin to complain? It was his fault, wasn't it, for not taking Pullpin's place on the chair, with the sharks? For thinking that he could exist without his twin?

Then it was their biggest show, in the heart of Texas, the tent so big and tattered that the holes in the top seemed like stars in reverse, points of dark in a sea of light. There were thousands there to see the act, and Pushpin knew they were there to see him die. Would it be the one-ton weight hovering over the tray of cupcakes that would get him? Would it be the enormous bear trap Pullpin had set up around a soft recliner in the center of the stage? Would Pullpin goad the audience into a frenzy that would descend and render Pushpin's body as red as his honking nose?

Pushpin staggered into the ring to the roar of applause. He carried a bucket of water and a rag. Pullpin lingered out of sight, perhaps curious at this deviation from script. Pushpin stopped, pushed the rag into the water, brought it to his face. He scrubbed — scrubbed away the clown until all that stood before the crowd was a man.

Afterward, no one could quite agree what he looked like. What color was his skin? Was he tall or short? Did he still have that painted star above his left eye? All anyone could agree on was that, in his face, they all seemed to recognize something. If only in the gaunt expression he wore, everyone knew him in that moment when the clown was gone, the moment before he walked over to the cupcakes and picked one up.

Afterward, most people would admit that they had forgotten about the weight dangling above him. They were too lost in the hope on his face, in how much they wanted him to bring the small pink mass to his lips and taste it. They were all, for once, Pushpin in that moment. They were brought back to themselves by the snap of rope and crunch of bone. And a single haunting voice laughing maniacally, no longer one of a pair, no longer much of anything.

One by one the audience began to stand and walk away. Pullpin continued in the ring, but alone he was worse than annoying. The link was broken. Did he finally disappear when the last person left? Did he finally pass on? No one is sure, as no one looked back to check. But no one is haunted by not knowing. Some have, however, started painting little stars above their left eyes.

❀

113

Fact: Clowns cannot smell **fear**.
They smell ultraviolet bands of light,
the winds of change,
and **causality**.
Liars give them sinus infections.

Clowns of the Creosote Plains
by Chillbear Latrigue

When everything that you care about becomes a radioactive ball of plasma, it changes your perspective on things. Like when I say, "Our clown car is rocketing across the wasteland," you probably imagine a really sweet souped up jalopy, stuffed full of classic big top mimes all dressed in brightly colored regalia, burning two dark lines in the hardpan. Not anymore. What I'm talking about is the piece of shit MINI Cooper that we covered in lead-based paint like a goddamn Romero Britto suitcase rattling along at 30 mph across the flat, dead gravel that used to be condos and shopping malls.

We use hyperbole because reality is terrible. We paint grins on our faces because a sad clown no longer has a place in this post-apocalyptic world.

Water, food, fuel, weapons, and women, in that order. We would occasionally play with other words to try to make it the "Five Ws" or the "Five Fs" of survival, but nothing fit, so we settled for the awkward abbreviation of WFFWW, creating another hardship.

Bingo has the wheel, and I'm riding shotgun. All clowns love packing a MINI, but the front is really the place we want to be. It has cachet. Honestly, though, we're a wretched lot. The fanciful polka dots painted on the men's hazmat suits are so dust covered and faded that they looked like they're just wearing plain hazmat suits, lacking in any whimsy. Only, Zippy, Loafer, and the Brick have any makeup on, and theirs is so splotchy you can see their radiation scars. "Put your mother-fucking noses on," I shout. The surest way to lose control over a clown troupe is to allow discipline to falter. They aren't just noses; they're who we are. Hunger, thirst, and fear are pervasive. We need these red balls as much as we need WFFWW.

"Keep your eyes on those windows, boys. I got a big feelin'," Bingo says. "Y'all got 'Lucky B drivin.'" Bingo talks a big game about being the lucky driver, but there's little evidence to support the claim. Someone blows a horn.

Fact: Clowns are the most braggadocious of all apocalyptic survivors.

Bingo is competent behind the wheel, at best.

Reflective surfaces catch our attention. It's not that clowns are intrinsically drawn to shiny objects — that's a myth. Important things shine in the sun: metal, glass, water, and even the occasional weapon pointed our way. I notice a gleam maybe five miles to the right of the clown car. North.

A flash of light doesn't mean that we go thundering — at 30 mph, mind you — to its point of origin. Fuel is precious and traps abound. Chase after glimmers and you'll find yourself eaten by mutants or dead from radiation exposure. Still, some of us are impatient and don't want to waste time, so we ask the Wise Clown. The Wise Clown says wait, and so we do.

It's about two hours before dusk, so we kill the engine and take turns clown napping, which is the same as regular napping, only in this case, the nappers are clowns.

As darkness envelops the plain, the reflective glare continues to flicker and fade until it's replaced by the pale light of a campfire, the sight of which infects the clown troupe with nervous energy. The brutal night air will soon arrive, so we only have about an hour of darkness before conditions become unbearable. Jackie takes his turn at the wheel and the MINI crawls toward the strangers. We apply polka dots to our garments and fresh makeup to our faces. The car stops about a thousand yards out behind some scrub. We exit the vehicle in true clown fashion, and assume a practiced tactical formation. Tactics are important as our weaponry is limited to traditional clowning implements: bulbous horns; squirting flowers, juggling balls, oversized blunderbusses loaded with confetti and flags that say "BANG!," and a few unicycles for lightning fast movement.

Fact: Floppy clown shoes are quiet on the hardpan, but make a distinctive sound on creosote. Special care must always be taken.

As we near the site, we count half a dozen survivors around the fire. There are also two motorcycles and a horse a few yards away — rare prizes in the new age. The strangers are armed with rifles and holstered handguns.

Zipper and the Brick, both armed with blunderbusses, fan out to the right and left. Two other clowns mount unicycles and ride in opposite directions to circle to the other side of the fire. In a few moments, these vagabonds will be surrounded. If possible, we will not harm the campers or eat their horse; but anything could happen during initial contact, and it's not like we *wouldn't* eat the horse. We just want things to be on our terms.

Our movements are swift and flawless, and the success of this mission seems assured, until someone honks his horn prematurely.

What occurs in the first few seconds can only be described as bedlam. Like spokes on a wagon wheel, shots arc outward from the hub. I shout "CLOWN ANTICS!" and we begin our merry dance of death. Some tumble, some juggle, and some just bound up to our reluctant audience and laugh hysterically. One by one, though, we fall to the ground.

Those who aren't hurt badly continue the routine. Zipper tries to use a blunderbuss to support his weight, but falls to the ground. He manages to level the weapon at our assailants, and sprays them with a brightly colored blast of confetti. One of the strangers responds by pointing a revolver at the hapless clown, but fires on an empty chamber. Zipper would eventually succumb to his wounds, and he isn't the only one. We lose three clowns, and four others suffer leg amputations. Their severed limbs will later be replaced with hilarious stilts.

When the smoke clears, the strangers admit, while initially alarming, ours is the best post-holocaust clown act they've seen. They ask to join our menagerie, and as if by magic, the clown troupe expands from twelve to fifteen.

Fact: A clown will never admit that a car is full.

This story is dedicated to Zipper, Stuffy, and the Brick.

Fact: Balloons are a vital food source for clowns. They are tied in intricate knots before **slaughter** (e.g. animal shapes) to prevent escape.

Fact: Cheetahs can reach up to 62 MPH in pursuit of their **prey**. Clowns can reach 70.

A Distant Honk

by Holly Schofield

The footprints were as big as my snowshoe, the crisp outline of the heel signifying a clown shoe, the impression not more than a couple of hours old.

The tracks beelined from the forest edge toward my campsite, then grew more erratic as they disappeared between dark spruce trees hunched under their winter burdens. I shuddered, picturing the clown stumbling through last night's snowy darkness: hands flapping in the cold, grinning fiercely, a low hoot escaping its winter-roughened lips. With my heavy down sleeping bag pulled over my head, I hadn't heard a sound, relying on the campfire to keep away predators.

I plodded to where the tracks entered the clearing, the slush sticking to my snowshoes. The sun had risen above the mountaintops, warm for February, warmer than all previous weather records.

A clump of coarse orange hair clung to a hemlock twig, sodden with mud. The email from the game warden had been accurate — the clowns *had* left hibernation early, the earliest yet, the unusually high temperatures triggering abnormal metabolic changes.

The troupe's cave would be much farther up the mountain. I pictured melting ice dripping off the cave ceiling, streaking their greasepaint as they lay curled around one another like rats in a nest. With blank expressions and creaking joints, they'd unfold themselves, straighten their faded blouses on their too-lean frames, and honk softly. Then, they'd burst forth from the cave, one after another after another in astonishing numbers, bewildered by the bright sunshine, wanting to sate their terrible hunger.

What could one biologist do? I'd soon finish my dissertation on the wild clowns' shrinking range but there could be no future in coulrology. Since my study had begun, frown lines had etched an oval around my mouth.

At my campsite, I methodically stuffed a daypack for the trip up the mountains. The rest of the gear and food went into my larger backpack. I hefted it, looking for a suitable branch to suspend it from, to keep it safe until I returned. A small bag tumbled out, yellow kernels gleaming beneath plastic packaging. My reserve food, my comfort food. I picked it up slowly.

I put the last of the logs on the remnants of yesterday's fire, although I'd return tired and cold tonight. I fed in scraps of wood until flames fingered up. The last of the butter coated the cooking pot and softened the clinking sound the kernels made as they bounced. A puff of acrid smoke crept out from beneath the lid and I shook the pan harder. I should have waited for coals but, then, patience is not one of humankind's virtues.

Walking in snowshoes takes practice and constant attention to detail. I managed to drink from my water bottle without stopping, juggling the container from hand to hand as I brushed aside wet branches and forged on upwards, inserting my feet into the softening footprints.

My dissertation advisor was convinced that wild clowns would be extinct by 2030. She wanted me to change to cockroach studies and offered to line up space station projects. Her voice rang in my head, drowning out the muttering birds and creaking branches. You can't base a career on a dying species. Don't back a loser. *Get out while you can.*

I grew warm, opening the ear flaps on my fur-lined hat, letting the breeze flip them up.

As I hiked, hemlock gave way to spruce which shrank in stature but not in age. Did a hundred-year-old tree have more wisdom than a sapling? I hoped so. I hoped humankind was gaining more than bare knowledge as it slaughtered thousands of species and chased thousands of others into unsuitable environments.

Wild clowns had their own niche in the ecosystem and every right to perform as nature intended. Every right to hibernate, arise, and eat their fill. Suddenly chilled, I drew my ear flaps close again.

The increasingly slushy tracks zigzagged through the undergrowth, always uphill. Sometimes a slip of the foot made my snowshoes clang together like a bell. Once, a rabbit dashed in front of me and I windmilled my arms, barely keeping my balance on the steep slope.

The hike gave me a chance to think, to ruminate on the crazy swirling globe we call home. I watched clouds skidding across the sky and pictured the world's animals and people as if we were all under one gigantic blue canvas roof. It didn't matter if climate change was man-made or not, clowns would soon parade out of the tent behind woolly mammoths and dodo birds. My future children would only ever see clowns in captivity.

I threw a snowball straight up and caught it. At this moment, caught in time until the terrain levelled, I could pretend it wasn't so.

The afternoon wind slapped my face as I entered the high meadow. Tracks of varying size and depth criss-crossed the snowy expanse. A curving, wide-mouthed cave entrance slashed through the rock face beyond. My drying sweat made me shiver.

A raven honked. I jumped and then made myself turn a deliberate circle, my overlapping tracks creating a daisy pattern in the snow. No wide white teeth gleamed, no broad half-moon eyes stared at me from the dim forest. The troupe should be far away, hunting until dawn.

The wind increased. I took a quick population estimate from the tracks, not even measuring out a plot, anxious to get back before dark.

That distinctive smell — a mixture of musk, decaying rubber, and decomposing sawdust — billowed out of the low cave. At the dirt-littered entrance, I awkwardly knelt in my bulky parka and snowshoes, then hesitated. I could stick my head in. But why take the risk? The clowns would need me in one piece if I was to be their spokesperson.

From far above, a distant hoot sounded, low and long, silencing the chatter of the birds.

I pulled the filled baggie from my daypack and gently shook it out on a rock by the entrance. As I headed back downhill, I glanced back at the mound of popcorn — unsure if it was a placation, a gift, or an admission of guilt.

Fact: Bifurcating a clown along a **pale** ring
will not cause two clowns to grow.
However, it causes the halves to enter their
mating cycle.

Postscript:
First and Last and Always

In 1802, Joseph Grimaldi, a promising young Clown following in his father's footsteps in the age-old tradition of the pantomime, made some radical changes to his costume, adding garish diamonds and circles to it, and applying elaborate makeup to his face. In the harlequinades of the time, Clown was a low-class buffoon, dressed in tatty servants' clothes, the comic idiot foil of the sly Harlequin. Clown embodied the concept that the lower classes were, in fact, stupid, graceless, and incompetent. With tassels and greasepaint, Grimaldi's 'Joey the Clown' permanently transformed the role — the character and personality — of Clown, making him the source of clever, mischievous pranks as often as he was the butt of them, and in doing so, changed the role of Harlequin, as well, presaging the overturning of the old social order, the permanent class system that defined people almost entirely by their social status, by aristocratic lineage, and the amount of money one's ancestors commanded.

Joseph Grimaldi died in relative obscurity, physically debilitated from multiple Clowning injuries, steeped in alcohol, depressed, and impoverished in that uniquely British way that restricts a person to having only a single servant.

Joey the Clown lives on.

When we put out our call for clown-themed fiction for our 2015 April Fools' Day issue, we expected silly, frilly stories. Killer Clowns. Wereclowns. Clownpires. It was a to be a silly, frilly mini-issue, after all.

And we received Killer Clowns, and Wereclowns, and Clownpires. But we got so much more: stories that explored both humor and fear, yes, but also loss, desire, rebellion, survival, redemption — the vast array of human emotion and experience revealed through a mask of greasepaint, and we knew that a mini-issue alone wouldn't do the clowns justice. A lark, a joke, took on a life of its own, and became the volume you hold now.

This, really, is where *Unlikely Story* started — as a joke. As something silly and audacious and too weird to work: *The Journal of Unlikely Entomology*. An online magazine of fiction about bugs. Who knew what could be done with bug stories?

Joey the Clown graced the stage for two decades, and then he was gone. But his DNA infiltrated the Clown, as it was, as it is, as it will be, changing the nature of Clowns and clowning forever.

This book stands as a culminating point, a point of transition, of change. An ending and a beginning. The magazine we ran since 2011 is financially unsustainable, and can't continue in its current form. *Clowns* is the period at the end of the sentence.

Or perhaps, the first word in the beginning of the next.

**Fact: there are always more clowns in the car
after the last one gets out.**

❀

Contributors

Jason Arias lives in Portland, OR with his wife and sons. He rarely turns down an opportunity to read or eat. His house is filled with books and food. He may have a problem. His work has appeared in *Perceptions Magazine, Blue Skirt Productions, Clockhouse,* and many other publications.

T. Jane Berry lives near Seattle. She writes science fiction, fantasy, and horror and can be found on Twitter @TJaneBerry.

Robin Blyn is Professor of English at the University of West Florida, where she teaches a variety of classes in twentieth century and contemporary literature and culture. Her first book, *The Freak-garde: Extraordinary Bodies and Revolutionary Art in America,* explores the many ways that avant-garde artists in the U.S. turn to the traditions of the freak show in order to imagine new ways of being. She is currently at work on a new book about neoliberalism and network aesthetics.

Dayle A. Dermatis has been called "one of the best writers working today" by *USA Today* bestselling author Dean Wesley Smith. Under various pseudonyms (and sometimes with coauthors), she's sold multiple novels and more than a hundred short stories in various genres, including fantasy, science fiction, erotica, romance, thriller, and YA. A recent transplant to the amazingly green Pacific Northwest, in her spare time she follows Styx around the country and travels the world, all of which inspires her writing. She loves music, cats, Wales, old houses, magic, laughter, and defying expectations. To find out where she is today, check out www.DayleDermatis.com.

By day, **Evan Dicken** studies old Japanese maps and crunches data on all manner of amazing medical experiments at The Ohio State University. By night, he does neither of these things. His work has most recently appeared in: *Shock Totem*, *Analog*, and *Daily Science Fiction*, and he has stories forthcoming from publishers such as: *Pseudopod*, *The Lovecraft eZine*, and *The Overcast*. Feel free to drop by at: evandicken.com.

Cate Gardner recently moved to the wilds of the Wirral although from certain vantage points, she can still see her beloved Liverpool. Her stories have appeared in many weird and wonderful places such as *The Journal of Unlikely Entomology*, *Shimmer*, *Black Static*, *Postscripts* and *Shock Totem*. Her fifth novella, *The Bureau of Them*, was published this summer by Spectral Press and she has a mini collection forthcoming with Frightful Horrors. You can find her on the web at www.categardner.net

Line Henriksen lives in the cold, darks depths of Sweden, where there is no hope and no shops open on Sundays. Her work has appeared in *theEEEL* by tNY.Press, *freeze frame fiction* and *Pankhearst's Slim Volume: Wherever you Roam*.

Cassandra Khaw is Ysbryd Games' business cat and an occasional contributor in Ars Technica UK. Her short fiction can be found at places like *Shimmer*, *Terraform*, *The Dark*, and *Mythic Delirium*. She has a novella coming out with Abaddon Books sometime Soon.

Chris Kuriata lives in the Niagara Region. As well as editing TV programs about murderers, faith healers, and hockey, his short fiction has appeared in many fine magazines like *Taddle Creek, Grain*, and *Phobos*. His work will appear in the upcoming Exile anthology *The Playground of Lost Toys*.

Chillbear Latrigue is the pen name for M.F. Davis, a founding contributor and editor at Portland's celebrated *Drunk in a Midnight Choir* blog. When not aggressively toiling to make raw, honest poetry, satire, and other literature more accessible to the literate masses, he dabbles in fighting crime as an American peace officer (working well within the established constitutional parameters of his profession). His passion is stringing together bunches of words to make what he hopes are coherent stories. Chillbear hangs his hat in a small burg in Broward County, Florida, but he hates it there — mostly due to the lack of indigenous hunting hawks. Follow him @Chillbear on Twitter and pretty much everything else that contains an @.

Derek Manuel lives in Louisiana where he earns a living by muttering dark and powerful incantations in broken Latin before a robed figure with a disapproving countenance. His historical notes on events better forgotten or prevented have appeared in the *Perpetual Motion Machine Publishing* newsletter and *The Drabblecast*.

Sara K. McNeilly typically gets graded for her writing but on occasion writes something that needs to be shared. She has written chapbooks in poetry and prose-poetry, and her work has appeared in the *Capilano Courier*. Sara has a BA in English Literature and a Certificate in Creative Writing from Simon Fraser University. She lives in Vancouver, sporadically updates her running blog, runths.wordpress.com, and shows occasional wit on twitter (@sarasitic)

Virginia M. Mohlere was born on one solstice, and her sister was born on the other. Her chronic writing disorder stems from early childhood. She lives in the swamps of Houston and writes with a fountain pen that is extinct in the wild. Her work has been seen in *Cabinet des Fées*, *Jabberwocky*, *Lakeside Circus*, *Goblin Fruit*, *Strange Horizons*, and *MungBeing*. http://www.virginiamohlere.com/

A personal trainer by day, **Joe Nazare** spends his nights working to get readers bent all out of shape. His fiction, poetry, and nonfiction has appeared in such places as *Dark Discoveries*, *Pseudopod*, *Damnation Books*, *Shroud*, *Lovecraft eZine*, *The Zombie Feed—Vol I.*, *Grievous Angel*, *Star*Line*, *The Internet Review of Science Fiction*, and *Butcher Knives & Body Counts: Essays on the Formula, Frights, and Fun of the Slasher Film*. He is also the author of the collection *Autumn Lauds: Poems for the Halloween Season*.

Mari Ness lives in central Florida. Her work has also appeared in *Tor. com*, *Clarkesworld*, *Daily Science Fiction*, *Apex Magazine*, *Uncanny*, and *Unlikely Story*. She twitters about nothing in particular at mari_ness. She quite likes clowns.

Charles Payseur currently resides in Wisconsin, where his partner, a gaggle of pets, and more craft beer than is strictly healthy help him through the long winters. His work has appeared or is forthcoming at *Strange Horizons*, *Nightmare Magazine*, and in *Lightspeed Magazine's Queers Destroy Science Fiction*. You can find him around the internet as contributor to a number of sites and on his blog, *Quick Sip Reviews* (www.quicksipreviews.blogspot.com), as well as on Twitter as @ ClowderofTwo.

J.H. Pell lives in Michigan with a variety of other mammals, and has probably just made *another* cup of tea.

Bryan Prindiville is currently an Art Director for Catholic Relief Services (CRS) where he has also worked as a designer and illustrator since late 2000. In his free time he has had a hand in a number of webcomics including *Bassetville* and *Hello with Cheese*. Traditionally published work can be found in *Rum and Runestones* and Tee Morris' *All a Twitter* and others. Less traditionally he can be found as a member of the live art entertainment show Super Art Fight. More information and work are available at his sketch blog, bryanprindiville.com.

Kristen Roupenian is a writer living in Ann Arbor, Michigan. Her short stories can be found in *The Weird Fiction Review* and elsewhere.

Holly Schofield tries to adapt to whatever environment she finds herself in and hopes she ultimately provides a net benefit to her microhabitat. Her stories have appeared in many publications including *Lightspeed*, *Crossed Genres*, and *Tesseracts*. For more of her work, see http://hollyschofield.wordpress.com/

Carlie St.George is a Clarion West graduate whose work has appeared or is forthcoming in *Lightspeed*, *Strange Horizons*, *Shock Totem*, and *Shimmer*. Her snarky movie reviews can be found at mygeekblasphemy. com. While not especially afraid of clowns, she admits she'd probably react poorly if she came across one in the middle of the night.

Jeff Wolf was born and raised in suburban Chicago. He currently lives on the North Side, where he does freelance advertising work to support his fiction habit. He has a degree from Marquette University.

Karlo Yeager Rodríguez was born and raised on the enchanted island of Puerto Rico, but chose to move to Baltimore, Maryland a few years back. When not answering questions, like, "Why Baltimore?" he works on accessibility issues, and finds time to write. He has a healthy respect for clowns, but not a fear, because he's sure that if he runs across one in its natural habitat it is more afraid of him than he is of it. His fiction has appeared in the Autumn 2014 issue of *PULP Literature*, and his science fiction book reviews can be found in the *Pittsburgh Post Gazette*. His sporadic witticisms can be found on twitter (@kjy1066).

Caroline M. Yoachim lives in Seattle and loves cold cloudy weather. She is the author of dozens of short stories, appearing in *Lightspeed*, *Asimov's*, *Clarkesworld*, and *Daily Science Fiction*, among other places. Her debut short story collection, *Seven Wonders of a Once and Future World & Other Stories*, is coming out with Fairwood Press in 2016. For more about Caroline, check out her website at http://carolineyoachim.com

Credits and Acknowledgements

Kickstarter

This book would have been impossible without the generous support of our backers. Very special thanks to all of you.

- Lew Andrada
- Rebecca J. Allred
- Charlotte Ashley
- Steph P. Bianchini
- Justin Biegel
- Jennifer Bohatch
- Gregory Norman Bossert
- Amy Bush
- @CheffoJeffo
- Andrew D'Apice
- Scott Dicken
- http://WhoLovesYou.ME
- B.L. Draper
- Anne M. Gibson
- A.T. Greenblatt
- Daniel Jacobs

- Merry Jones
- Andrew Kaye
- Anna Kashina
- Anon
- Bruce Konefsky
- Ed Kratz
- Ron Mansolino
- Marnie
- Anonymous
- Ed McNamara
- Virginia M. Mohlere
- Paul Mojzes
- Rajiv Mote
- Erik Newman
- K.A. Rochnik
- Carol Roupenian
- Kristen Roupenian
- Signe Saboe
- Michael and Joy Scoble
- Jason Sizemore
- Mary Spila
- Mekaela St. George
- Clive Tern
- Patrick Thomas
- Samuel J Tomaino
- Deborah Walker

- Brook West
- Brian White
- Sylvia Spruck Wrigley
- Isabel Yap

Clown Facts

When it comes to research, the Internet is a profound tool. While we were aware of some of the more esoteric facts about clowns, the encyclopedic knowledge presented in this volume is the product of the aggregate wisdom of the net. We'd like to acknowledge those people whose deep understanding of that most mysterious of sub-species, the clown, has so enriched this volume.

- Andy Brown
- Luke McKinney
- Charles Payseur
- Jes Rausch
- Steve Toase
- Donald Jacob Uitvlugt
- Doree Weller
- John Wiswell

We would also like to thank Shriekback for providing the music for our Kickstarter video, and to Gregory Norman Bossert for setting images to the music. Additional thanks to A.T. Greenblatt for her assistance with the video, and to Cynthia Baumann, who has been proofreading for *Unlikely Story* since we were a little baby 'zine.

❀

Fact: There's **nothing** you can do.
In the **end**, the clowns will still come for you.
They always do.

http://www.unlikely-story.com